The Christmas
Mrs Capper's
David W Robinson

© David W Robinson 2023

Edited by Maureen Vincent-Northam
Cover Design Rhys Vincent-Northam

Prologue

Hello and welcome to Christine Capper's Comings & Goings, your weekly vlog on what's been happening in and around Haxford, brought to you this week by Haxford Brewery, the finest ales in the Haxford vales.

Haxford Recorder: December 16

Local personality, Christine Capper, known throughout Haxford for her weekly vlog and her interviews on Radio Haxford, was arrested in the early hours of this morning suspected of killing Katya Watkins during the Haxford Christmas Festival Ball at Barncroft's Farm last night.

Ms Watkins, a checkout supervisor at CutCost, was found strangled close to the temporary toilets at about 10:15 last night, and initial inquiries led Detective Inspector Patrick Quinn of West Yorkshire CID to take Mrs Capper in for questioning on suspicion of committing the crime.

"We have been speaking to a woman concerning last night's event. She is currently

1

helping with our inquiries, and I'm sorry, but I can't say any more than that at this moment."

The suspect was later identified as Christine Capper.

We'll bring you updates on this story as it develops.

So read the headline on the front page of the Haxford Recorder as I read it on the cold, damp, and grim Saturday afternoon after the Friday night ball. The report did nothing to lift my spirits. Yes, I was at the Christmas Ball, yes, I saw the poor woman, yes, I had crossed swords with her earlier in the day and the previous day, and yes, I was working on a case that might have involved her if only on the periphery, but no: as God is my judge, jury, and executioner, I did not kill her.

That terrible Friday night/Saturday morning would have far reaching effects for me, and as always it came about not entirely by chance, but not by design either. I have to say that the catalyst came a few days earlier from Eric Reitman my producer/director at Radio Haxford.

But first, let me take you back to Monday, December 11, two weeks before Christmas, when quite by chance I made a new friend.

Chapter One

They say that most animals are impervious to the weather. They don't worry about it. They don't pine for glorious sunshine the way we humans do. The weather just is.

Whoever told you that, didn't know Cappy the Cat. When I opened the conservatory door to a windy, rainy, and icy cold December Monday morning, he shot out, leapt over the fence into the Timmins's back garden to attend to his ablutions, and was back inside two minutes, glowering up at me for having the audacity to make the weather so bad. Even putting down a feed for him did nothing to appease his annoyance. He wolfed it down and rather than thanking me, or even acknowledging my servile duties by curling himself around my legs, he trotted back into the front room where he would snuggle down in his bed or in front of the fire… or not considering the fire was off.

And he wouldn't be there for long. Barry Snodgrass, known to everyone but me as Snoddy (I didn't approve of nicknames but everyone else in Haxford did) was due within the hour to start work on that same front room, and for the three days that he was in residence Cappy the Cat would be living with Dennis and me in the kitchen and conservatory.

He decorated our kitchen earlier in the year (Barry, that is, not Cappy the Cat) and if that was the subject of some argument between Dennis and me, it was nothing compared to the grumbling my other half did at the potential cost of brightening up the front room.

"Eight hundred nicker?" he protested when Barry left us the estimate. "What you gonna do? Rebuild the house from the damp course up?"

To me it was a reasonable price. It was a large room and the walls needed stripping, the woodwork needed repainting, so did the ceiling, and then there was re-papering, which would take a full day to complete. I chose the paper, naturally. A sort of café-au-lait with random squares in a darker colour and little, silver squiggles here and there. Sober and pleasant on the eye. Barry charged us £25 a roll and I needed eight rolls. Beyond that, I also insisted on an architrave right round the room. That added another £100 to the bill, and if all Dennis anticipated was the bill, I was looking forward to the finished job.

Naturally, there were problems. It wouldn't be a Capper job if there weren't. The biggest hurdle we would face was keeping Cappy the Cat out of the room until the paint dried. Dennis did the job the last time we decorated, and Cappy the Cat's coat was naturally black and white, but he ended up with rather more white than he had when we started.

Beyond that potential problem, I hadn't been able to start with my Christmas decorations. Normally, I would set about that job on December 1st, but now it would be the end of the week, the

16th, before I could even put up my tree. I usually put lights round the front window, too, but I daren't even do that in case they got in Barry's way.

Dennis's considerations were much more mundane. For the next three or four nights he had to watch *Bangers & Cash* on his laptop in the conservatory. You have to feel sorry for him. Well, you don't. I mean, I never do.

Radio Haxford was another area of Christmas concern for me. According to the great god listener ratings, the Christine Capper Interview was doing well but right now, the diary was empty until well into the New Year, and I recalled last year when without warning and just a few days before it was due to happen, Eric Reitman told me that over the two-day period at Christmas Manor, I would be delivering not one but two programmes in front of a live audience. Thanks to a resident murderer, it didn't quite work out how he imagined, but I could still recall the dread I felt when I sat before that invited audience and told them all about the Graveyard Poisoner.

Surely I had matured since then, you ask. Well, not so you'd notice but that was because we hadn't done a live broadcast since (other than my weekly agony aunt spot) and we certainly hadn't done anything in front of an audience.

I had, however, given a talk to a class of 16-year-olds on the truth about life as a private investigator. It was politely received, but I couldn't detect any great enthusiasm amongst those teenagers, and their level of interest was summed up when one boy asked, "Do you, like, get to, you know, shine any bad guys on?" and the rest of the class, girls included, murmured their approval of the idea.

I came away with the thought that television (mostly but not exclusively of the American variety) had much to answer for.

It was when I gave that talk that I first met Joanne Petheridge, who liked to be called Jo.

About my age, slimmish, with short, neatly styled, black hair and intense green eyes, she was a teaching assistant, one of those dogsbodies who help the teacher, help the students, help the school's image, help everything and everyone but themselves. She wasn't really needed that afternoon, but as she explained at the time, she had nothing better to do on a wet Wednesday in November, and after the job was over, I had a cup of tea and chat with her in the staff room. I drove away and never saw nor heard from her again.

Famous last words. With the clock reading a few minutes past nine, as I sat in the kitchen anticipating Barry Snodgrass turning up to start work on the front room, the doorbell rang and I rushed to answer it, confidently expecting to greet Barry clad in his white overalls and carrying his dust sheets. But it wasn't him. It was Jo, shrouded in a parka and shivering in the rain.

And she was as surprised to see me as I was to see her. "Oh, hullo, Christine. I didn't realise you lived here."

"Jo. Lovely to see you again, but I was actually expecting someone else." I smiled. "What can I do for you?"

"Well, I'm your neighbour's new carer." She gestured to Hazel's next door. "Mrs McQuarrie?"

"Oh. I see." I didn't really. What was a teaching assistant doing moonlighting as a carer? And during term time, if you please?

Jo pressed on. "I've rung the bell, and I can't get an answer."

"You won't. She's in the Balearics… I think. A pre-Christmas break in the sun… Oh, look at me forgetting my manners. Come in out of the cold, and let me get you a cup of tea… or are you due in school?"

"School is no longer a factor. Believe it or not, I was made redundant. Not that I was too worried. A lot of stress in that job." She returned a wan smile. "You know how it is."

"I do." I stood back to let her in, took her coat and spread it over the radiator to let it dry, then led her through to the conservatory, where I sat her close to that room's single radiator while I went back to the kitchen to make tea for both of us.

People often say I'm nosy. My argument is that it goes with the private eye territory. It wasn't exclusive to me, though. Cappy the Cat was just as inquisitive, even if slightly more parochial in that he only poked his nose into events at our house rather than the rest of Haxford. I didn't see him (not that he would care if I did) but I knew that he would be in the conservatory checking out our visitor on the offchance that she might feed him. He was the same with all callers. Even the man who used to read the gas and electricity meters in the days before we got a smart meter was subjected to Cappy the Cat's

7

scrutiny.

When I returned to the conservatory armed with tea and chocolate digestives, he was there, sitting on Jo's lap, purring contentedly. But that purr masked a laser stare aimed at me, which clearly said, "I am the master of this house – no I don't want to hear any argument – I am the master and this is the kind of attention I expect."

I settled opposite Jo, invited her to help herself, snatched a chocolate digestive, and said, "I'm expecting a decorator so we might be interrupted at any time."

"Oh. Right. I wondered why I didn't see any Christmas decs. Who are you using?"

"Barry Snodgrass." I glanced irritably at the clock. "If he ever gets here."

"It'll be the weather holding him up. A lot of traffic coming through town." Brightening a little, she said, "I know Barry. He'll do you a top class job."

I gestured back at the kitchen. "He did that for us. Back in the summer. Not too expensive, either."

She chuckled. "My other half always complains about the cost. Is yours like that?"

"Aren't they all? I'll tell you something, Jo. If I paid sixpence for something and Dennis could get it for fourpence, he'd still moan about the extra tuppence." I took a wet of tea. "You said there was a lot of stress in your job? I'm surprised. I wouldn't have thought you'd get much of that as an assistant?"

She too, took a biscuit. "Oh, you wouldn't believe it, Christine. You're at everyone's beck and

8

call, and the kids… Dear me. My name's Petheridge, but they called me anything and everything from beverage to leverage, and even haemorrhage. I think the worst was miscarriage. And they say kids don't understand poetry. They certainly knew how to come up with rhymes for me. And it's not like they did it behind my back. They'd actually call me those names to my face. I spent half my time giving them a severe talking to."

I sympathised. "I had similar problem when I first got married. I was a police officer at the time, and everyone started calling me Capper the Copper… including my colleagues."

She tutted. "It's the way it is these days, isn't it? Anyway, redundancies were on the table. Ancillary staff only. When all's said and done, they can't do without the teachers, can they? I talked it over with Bernard – that's my husband – and he suggested I take it and become a lady of leisure. I was actually working my notice when you came to the school to speak to the kids."

"I remember you telling me about Bernard. He's a plumber or something, isn't he?"

She nodded as she gulped down tea. "Works for Mallinson's, Sheffield road. They have a big contract with the council and Bernard makes top notch wages. Your Dennis probably knows him because Haxford Fixers service Mallinson's vans." She shrugged as she put her cup down. "Anyway, with my redundancy money we're fairly comfortable, so it's not like we needed a second income, but I found sitting round the house all day mind-numbing, so here I am, a former teaching assistant, now a carer."

"With an agency?"

"No. It's a private arrangement. You know Hazel's daughter, Belinda, do you?"

I confirmed it with a grim face. "Yes. For years. She was forever trying to get Hazel to leave Bracken Close and move in with her and her husband. Hazel always refused. But I thought Belinda lived over Leeds or Manchester or somewhere."

"Rochdale. She's our age. Early fifties. We went to school together and I bumped into her in Haxford a week or two back. She must have been calling on Hazel. I happened to mention I was technically out of work, she suggested I get in touch with Hazel and see about coming in two or three days a week for shopping, cleaning and stuff. Belinda will be paying and she promised me she'd mention it to Hazel. Last I heard, Hazel was all for it, but I haven't heard anything since, so I thought I'd call this morning and try and get the arrangements made." Her face fell. "And you say she's away on holiday?"

I nodded. "Majorca. Well, it's either Majorca or Morecambe. I think more likely Majorca. No one in their right mind would go to Morecambe at this time of year, would they?"

She laughed. "Not with Majorca on the table." Her face became more serious. "You don't know when she's due back?"

"Tomorrow, I think, but I don't know whether it's early afternoon or late night. They seem to be the only options from Manchester Airport. Tell you what, why don't you give me your number and let me bell you when I know?"

"You don't mind?"

"Couse not. I'm on Radio Haxford tomorrow morning. I am every Tuesday, but I'm usually home for half past twelve."

We exchanged numbers and as silence fell, I cast another glance at the clock. "Where on earth has Barry got to?"

"I told you, it'll be the traffic." Worry etched itself into her face. "I'm not holding you up, am I?"

"Not on a Monday," I told her with a genial smile. "Tuesday is my nightmare day. I have to be at Radio Haxford by half past ten to deliver the agony aunt slot at eleven. The only item on my schedule today is our Mr Snodgr—"

Right at that moment, the doorbell cut me off and as I rose to answer it, my mobile rang.

"Typical. Sorry, Jo, could you be an angel and get the door for me?"

She nodded and made for the front door while I checked the menu of my smartphone. The number was there to be read but unknown to the phone. This was in keeping with most calls, especially those seeking the help of a private investigator.

I snatched up my notebook and pen (I always kept a set on the magazine shelf of the conservatory coffee table) then swept a finger across the screen to make the connection and put the phone to my ear. "Christine Capper."

"Are you Capper?"

It was a woman's voice, but regardless of gender, everyone seemed to ask that question. It was as if they all assumed I employed a secretary.

"Yes, I'm Christine."

"Good, I need your help."

"In what capacity?"

"A private dick. What else?"

If I found the term 'private dick' offensive, my annoyance was aggravated by her tone. Plain spoken, pure Haxford, forceful and irritated.

"All right, First, may I ask who you are?"

"Adele Mottershaw. You're interviewing my husband for the radio next Monday."

This was news to me, but no doubt Eric Reitman would tell me all about it on Tuesday morning. "Am I?"

"So my old man tells me. Anyway, I need to see you because I've been robbed."

"Call the police."

It was my standard, opening gambit for any case where there was illegal activity.

As she replied, Jo and Barry Snodgrass came into the room. I heard him mention a bracelet, and nosy is as nosy does, I was suddenly listening to two conversations.

"There are reasons why I won't call the cops—
"

"Haven't seen anything of it, Barry—"

"—But I'm not prepared to talk about them over the phone—"

"—I'm sure it'll turn up."

"—Can you come and see me?"

Things got so confusing that I almost called her Mrs Bracelet, then Mrs Snodgrass, and even Mrs Jo, and it came out as "Of course, Mrs Bracesnodjo…"

before I checked myself and focussed on the caller. "It depends where you are. I mean if you're in Haxford, I can be there in an hour, but if—"

"Not today," she interrupted. "In fact, it won't be this side of Thursday or Friday because I have work to do."

"Fine. How about we say eleven o'clock Thursday morning?"

"Suits me. Let me give you the address."

I noted it down as she delivered it. "All right Mrs…" Again, I trailed off, but it wasn't confabulation this time. It was client confidentiality. The names of my clients were not for the listening ears of Jo Petheridge and Barry Snodgrass. "…Madam," I concluded lamely. "I'll see you Thursday morning."

I cut the call, folded away the piece of paper on which I'd written her name and address, and then smiled at my guests… well, one guest and one tradesman. "Sorry about that. Business. Hello, Barry. Raring to go are you?"

"Sorry I'm a bit late, Christine. Traffic's hell this morning."

"No problem. Want a brew before you start?"

"As long as it's all right with you, I'll have a brew as I start."

"Be my guest. Jo? Another cuppa?"

"Well, if you're sure…"

"Honestly, I'm glad of the company."

I passed a few minutes making tea for three, and while Barry made for the front room, I ensured that Cappy the Cat was locked out of his way and then joined Jo in the conservatory again. Our moody

13

moggie soon joined us. Not that he made his presence known. Unable to get to the front room, he simply sauntered in, ignored us, and settled down in a spare armchair.

"Was that Adele Mottershaw you were talking to?" Jo asked and took me by surprise.

"I can't really speak about clients, Jo. What makes you think it was her?"

"I could hear her talking and it sounded like her. Loud, brash, always sounds a bit ill-tempered. She's a part time, one-to-one teacher for the kids who are getting behind the rest of the class. Mainly English literature and language. She's a genuine firebrand and even the supposed tough kids dread working with her."

I made a mental note to put on my tough front when I met the woman, and then subtly – or not so subtly – changed the subject. "What was Barry saying about a bracelet?"

"I've lost it." Her face fell. "Bernard bought me it for my fiftieth birthday. Just a plain band, but it's nine carat gold, and he had it engraved on the inside. I can't find it anywhere. I mean, you don't wear that kind of stuff day to day, do you? I kept it for special occasions and the last time I recall wearing it was at a Halloween party given by some friends. I'm sure I had it when I got home, but I'm hanged if I can find it now." She shuddered. "Bernard went spare when he found out. I mean it cost him a fortune. Over two hundred pounds and I don't think our insurance covers that kind of loss."

I was slightly gobsmacked. Bernard paid two hundred plus for a bracelet. Dennis made an excellent salary from Haxford Fixers, but if he bought me a bracelet, even twenty-four carat gold (not that you could get that in Haxford) he'd go no higher than fifty.

I focused on Jo and determined to get to the root of all evil, asked, "So how did Barry know about it?"

"Bernard told him. They were working on a job together. A few weeks back." She appealed to my charitable nature. "I don't suppose you do lost property as a private eye, do you?"

I declined with a sad, sympathetic shake of the head. "Stolen property, sure, but it's really the province of the police. But lost property... it's a question of where it might have been lost, and if it was in the house, say, you'd end up paying me to do something you could do yourself."

Chapter Two

What I told Jo about my regular, Tuesday spot on Radio Haxford was the truth. What I didn't tell her was the level of... not exactly stress but certainly jangly nerves it created.

I had to be up early – it was necessary anyway because Barry was due again – I had to get breakfast out of the way, deal with both Dennis and Cappy the Cat, then get down to Haxford and into the studio for half past ten.

Studio was a grandiose name for the headquarters of Radio Haxford. Located on the upper Gallery of Haxford market hall, the place was actually an open plan office with a tiny soundproofed booth at the far end where the various presenters delivered their programmes.

At the time I arrived, that booth was occupied by Reggie Monk, the weekday morning anchor, complete with his general body odour and halitosis. In less than thirty minutes, I would join him to deliver my fifteen-minute, agony aunt slot, a regular highlight of Tuesday morning. A highlight for everyone else, that is, but having to share that shoebox with Reggie was the price I had to pay for my localised fame. More of a lowlight than a highlight.

Agony aunt was a phone in session, and I was obliged to get there half an hour early so that I could be briefed on any contentious issues which were likely to arise. Eric Reitman, our producer/director, quickly made it clear that the only issue the callers would likely bring up was the cost of the forthcoming Haxford Christmas Festival, and I wasn't allowed to comment upon it. I had my opinions the same as everyone else, usually prompted by the size of the Council Tax bill and the services we didn't get from the town hall, but I was obliged to keep them to myself. Such is the sacrifice of the radio presenter (part time).

I'd been doing it for a year and a half and then some, so I no longer felt nervous. If anything, I found it repetitive and occasionally boring. The questions were always the same, and so were the answers, but the job paid me about forty pounds. For an hour's work? The only way I could better that was working as a private eye, but as I've said so many times, Haxford was a small town and cases were few and far between. The Christine Capper Interview paid much more, but that was a once a week job (when we had interviewees lined up) and even then, we tended to record a couple at a time, so I could go a fortnight without having to turn one out. The agony aunt spot was weekly.

But it was also a hassle, and I was always glad to get it over and done with.

The Christine Capper Interview was another matter. After successful interviews with Georgie Tibbett and her sister Karen Dawkins, followed by another hour with former Haxford Town footballer,

17

Tel Wheatley, the Christine Capper Interview became an established highlight on Radio Haxford, riding high in the ratings and if Tel's complaints regarding veiled racism created something of a stir, it also generated a vibrant discussion on the station's website. I fervently wanted to throw in my two penn'orth, but as the presenter, I was obliged to maintain my neutrality and keep out of the debate other than posting the occasional 'thank you' on the comments which related to my performance.

Determined to build on our early success, Eric lined up a range of local notables (mercifully, Haxford was not big on genuine celebrities) and by the time we moved into October, our original schedule of one interview per fortnight had moved up a gear and we were on air every Sunday.

It meant more work for me, obviously but as Christmas approached I found myself totally confident and comfortable in the presence of such vaunted folk as Terry Shakespeare, the Mayor of Haxford, and Heather Connell, the head of Haxford Comprehensive (my old school). Eric also took the opportunity to drop the occasional bombshell on me, and given the current paucity of interviewees, he had one lined up for the morning of the 12th. This time, however, I was ahead of him thanks to Adele Mottershaw's call the previous day. Not that I realised it right away because his lead-in was out of left field.

What does that mean? Out of left field? I mean we have sheep and cattle all over the moors surrounding Haxford, and you could encounter them coming out of fields to your left or right, depending in which way you were facing when the stockman herded them.

I digress.

With our brief briefing over, we waited for the prompt for me to join Reggie in his cubbyhole, Eric asked, "How do you feel about the Haxford Larpers?"

I was slightly puzzled. Wrong, I was totally puzzled. "What in the name of jam and cream buns are Larpers?"

He laughed. "Larpers are people who indulge in LARP. L-A-R-P. It's an acronym for Live Action Role Play."

Eric was a nice man, happily married, not given to naughty, extramarital games, but all the same I wasn't sure I wanted to know what LARP meant. I'd been suspicious of acronyms ever since that morning when I answered the door to my son wearing only my nightie. I mean I was wearing the nightie, not Simon. He was so tall it would never fit him, and anyway, as a police officer, he would likely end up with a reputation he really didn't want. And talking of reputations, he told me to get dressed because I looked like MILF of the week. I didn't know what a MILF was and when I eventually found out, I was furious with Simon. Not only for describing me in such a derogatory manner, but also for knowing what it meant it the first place. Mind, he was twenty-six at the time, so maybe I was being a bit old-fashioned on the latter point. And I was certainly behind the door on the former. I mean, I understood acronyms like DIY and AKA, but MILF? And if LARP was Live Action Role Play, what kind of live action did these people have in mind, because if it was what I thought...

Still waiting for him to tell me that I would be interviewing Adele Mottershaw's husband, I had a blinding flash of insight which told me I was on the wrong track. Nothing unusual in that. "Oh. Right. I think I understand Live Action Role Play. You mean those people who re-enact famous battles of the Civil War? The Sealed Knot."

"Similar principle, granted, but these guys and gals get together every weekend in Hattersley Woods and act out their roles. And they take it seriously. No script or anything like that. They plan their tactics and then meet with the enemy. No quarter is asked, no quarter is given."

"Like paintballing?"

"Well, again, a similar sort of thing, but the Haxford Larpers play fantasy games, so they don't have guns. Just pointed hats, magic wands, and brooms for the witches. Right now, obviously, their games are based on Christmas."

"I see," I said, although I didn't really see anything that made sense. "I assume these are all adults. Not children."

"Correct, and we're lucky in that... you sound as if you don't approve, Chrissy."

I put on my innocent face. "No, no. Nothing of the kind. It's not my place to tell people how to lead their lives. I just think they could find more, er, constructive hobbies like..." I had to think about it. "Like realigning the bristles on toothbrushes. Still, I suppose I should be thankful that Dennis would never want to join them."

"He wouldn't?"

"Good lord, no; if the witches have brooms, they don't need cars, and I can't see Dennis being drawn to servicing their wands or potion mixing pots. Besides, as a true Yorkshireman, he'd want to cast spell to make sure his customers paid up without moaning about it. In fact, if you listen to some of his customers, he already has a magic wand. He uses it to jack the bill up." I had digressed enough, so I brought us back to the subject at hand. "So if these people are basing their games on Christmas, what do they do for the rest of the year?"

Eric shrugged. "Play the same games week after week, I assume." The fire began to burn in his eyes. "Anyway, you have an interview with one of them next Monday, the thirtieth. And not just one of them, but their leader, a chap named Heath Mottershaw. You know him?"

If I hadn't spoken to his wife the previous day, I might have thought Heath was his LARP name rather than the real McCoy. Answering Eric, I said, "In a roundabout way, yes. Listen, Eric, there's something you should know. Adele Mottershaw, this man's wife, rang me yesterday. I'm going to see her on Thursday in my private eye clothes. She's been robbed or something."

"That doesn't sound like it'll be a problem, Chrissy." His enthusiasm returned. "You haven't heard the good news yet. On Friday evening, you and a guest are invited to the Haxford Christmas Festival Ball at the old Barncroft Farm spread, on the edge of the Hattersley Woods."

This came as a surprise. I couldn't recall any

invitation coming through the post. "Me and a guest?"

"Well, the invitation was sent to Radio Haxford and it was left to us to choose who goes along. The big boss is unavailable, and when I put the proposition to Beryl, she turned it down flat." Beryl was his wife, deputy head in a comprehensive school somewhere the other side of Huddersfield. "It's coming up to the Christmas break," Eric went on, "and she's under pressure to make sure everything that's supposed to be finished really is one and dusted by Friday. That being the case, I thought of you and Dennis."

I was about to ask what on earth made him think of Dennis and me, but I never got the chance. Eric's daughter, Olivia, the office gopher (it was all she was fit for and even then she did an iffy job) was sending frantic signals that I was due in the booth with Reggie.

Although I say it myself, I was usually pretty cool and comfortable when handling the callers, but I was preoccupied with Eric's insistence that I represent Radio Haxford at the Christmas Festival Ball, as a result of which I made quite a few gaffes, not least of which was answering a question from a certain Mrs Ball seeking advice on her granddaughter's hyperactivity. I reassured her as best I could but I didn't tell her that I was in the same position. Now four years old, my granddaughter, beloved Bethany, was a similar bundle of irrepressible energy. I did, however address Mrs Ball as Mrs Christmas. Naturally, I apologised but Reggie, who fancied himself as a comedian, picked up on it when Mrs Ball rang off.

"Thanks for that, Mrs Festival. And our next caller is…"

It has been said that Reggie was the only one who fancied himself as a comedian. Regardless of my opinion that he was the unfunniest man in Haxford, I would never fancy him at all.

When my spot was through, I came out of the booth and received a short lecture from Eric on maintaining focus. I took it well, but I didn't entirely let him off the hook. "It was partly your fault. Telling me I'm going to the Christmas Festival Ball. Worse than that, I have to take Dennis."

"He won't like it?"

"I love my husband, Eric, but I have to be honest. He's not the most socially adroit man in Haxford. Why leave it at Haxford? He's not the most socially adroit man in the world. On the other hand, if the food and drinks are free, he'll be all for it, and he will be on his best behaviour, but within half an hour, he'll be boring the socks off people detailing the technical specifications of the model T Ford."

Once again, it was as if I had never said anything. "Radio Haxford sees this as a necessary public relations exercise, Chrissy, and you're the only one really set up to deal with it. At least you're married and you can take your husband along. Reggie's latest divorce has just come through, I can't really send Olivia, so who else is there?"

I had little choice but to give way. "All right. I'll do it, and don't worry about Dennis. He'll do it, too. Is it formal? You know. Evening gown for me, black tie for Dennis?"

"No. Nothing of the kind. In fact, it's fancy dress."

My heart sank so far so quickly that I'm sure I felt it drop into my shoes. "What?"

"Yes. You are obliged to turn up in fancy dress. The Larpers are putting on the show, but you don't have to follow their wizards and witches example. You go as whatever you want."

I groaned. "I have to hire some kind of fancy dress?"

"Yes, and don't forget to get the bill. Radio Haxford will pay for it. Hang on here, and I'll get the invitation for you."

Before I could protest he nipped upstairs for the invitation, and I sat down near the exit, and while I waited, I mulled the possibility of fancy dress.

It wasn't a particular problem for me. All those years ago, celebrating Millennium Eve, I hired a costume, and went to a party as Dorothy from the Wizard of Oz. The hire outfit came complete with black wig, a basket and toy Toto dog. I dressed Simon as a five-year-old Batman, and Ingrid as a two-year-old Sugar Plum Fairy. Dennis was the problem. He went to that party in his wedding suit, and his only nod to fancy dress was a 1930s-style black hat complete with white band, and he spent the evening insisting that he was dressed as Al Capone. He even borrowed my lipstick and drew a scar on his cheek, but few people were convinced.

I dreaded the thought of what he would make of a fancy dress party run by a gang of wizard and witch lookalikes.

Eric returned, and handed over the invitation. "We've pencilled your name in."

Pencilled nothing. My name was typed in.

A white card with pink edging, and various gold-coloured patterns, it read: *the Haxford Larpers extend a cordial invitation to Mrs Christine Capper* (that bit was typed in) *and guest to the Haxford Christmas Festival Ball at 7:30pm on Friday December 15th at the premises of Barncroft's Farm. Fancy dress obligatory.*

"Do I have to take a bottle?"

"No. Everything's laid on."

I groaned "Don't misunderstand me, Eric, but if this is a total disaster, it's down to you. I'll probably be okay with it, but as I said, it's Dennis."

"I'm sure he'll be fine."

Which demonstrated just how well he didn't know my mechanically obsessed other half.

Eric was still talking. "Of course, you don't have to take Dennis along. You could take someone else. A friend, perhaps."

I tried to think of a friend I might have who would be willing to make an absolute fool of him/herself. Val Wharrier was one option, but there was a problem with that; a problem called Dennis. Once he learned that there was an evening of free food and drink, the fancy dress and questionable entertainment wouldn't dissuade him. He'd be on his knees begging me to take him along.

Or would he?

Leaving the studio, I made my way (as I always did) to Terry's Tea Bar where mein host supplied the most divine toasted teacakes and tea, and as I sat with my light lunch, I tossed the options over in my mind.

A little over a year ago, two thugs beat Dennis quite badly, put him in hospital for several weeks, and he took months to recover. He was now back to full fitness, and at a shade under six feet, he had no fear of anyone or anything, a facet of his character which meant he never entertained the idea of tact. If anyone at a fancy dress party asked for his opinion of their costume, he would give it. 'You look a right prat' was about par for the course. Since I would be representing Radio Haxford, I would need to tape his mouth shut before we left home.

And with that in mind, it occurred to me that if I demanded he accompany me this coming Friday to Haxford Costume Hire on West Street, he would put up all sorts of objections, and even the prospect of free beer and buns that evening wouldn't be enough to make him miss an afternoon's work. The invitation said that we should be at Barncroft's Farm for half past seven, and given the state he usually came home in, i.e. filthy, covered in oil, grease, and the grime of an automotive workshop, he would have to finish work at four to get home, shower, shave and put on his costume. Dennis didn't like leaving work that early. He didn't like having to take a shower and shave either, but Haxford Fixers would be his overriding priority.

If this made me sound like a scheming wife, it was because where Dennis was concerned, I had to be a scheming wife. He had been a good husband for the better end of thirty years. Hard working, reliable, ever-ready to defend me in the face of criticism or threats, but he was also obsessed with the internal combustion engine and its associated mechanical iniquities to the exclusion of everything else, and that was something I could use.

By the time I left Terry's at half past twelve, Val Wharrier was looking more and more like my guest at the Christmas Festival Ball.

Chapter Three

As it turned out, she was a non-starter.

I got home about half past one, to be greeted by Cappy the Cat putting on his usual act of pain and starvation. The pain of betrayal because I had left him on his own for over three hours. He didn't even have Barry, who was busy in the front room, for company. And our crusty cat's impression of malnutrition was because he hadn't eaten since eight o'clock that morning when I last put a feed down for him.

He was very much like Dennis in many ways. Sulky when he didn't get his own way, capable of crawling all over you when it suited him, usually when there was something he wanted, determined to defend his territory against invaders from the local sparrow, starling, pigeon, and magpie clans, and entertaining complete disdain for Barbara and Fred Timmins. He regularly used their garden as the nearest lavatory. Not that Dennis used their garden as a toilet, but he didn't like the Timmins any more than Cappy the Cat liked them. They were far too snooty for Dennis or Cappy the Cat, and I had to agree with both my husband and our pet to some degree. Neither Fred nor Barbara had any cause to put on airs and graces. She was a pen pusher at

Haxford Comprehensive, and he was a similar pen pusher in one of the council departments.

Having dealt with our terrible tomcat, I settled in the conservatory with a cup of tea and a brace of chocolate digestives, and rang Val.

She was nothing if not apologetic. "To be honest, Chrissy, I was going to invite you as my guest."

"You mean you've been invited?" That didn't come out right. Even to me it sounded as if I was amazed that they would invite anyone as pointless as her. Still, perhaps she hadn't noticed.

"You don't have to sound so surprised. I'm working with the organiser, Heath Mottershaw, on a book about LARP."

"Sorry, Val. I didn't mean it like that. Truth is, I'll be representing Radio Haxford, and I was trying to think of someone I can take with me. Between you, me, and the gatepost, I don't really want to take Dennis."

"I'm in the same position with Tony. If I take him to a fancy dress party, he'll want a shirt that looks like a postage stamp, or worse, one that has an image of a postcard of Haxford, circa 1901 printed on the front."

Tony Wharrier was her husband, one of Dennis's business partners, and because of his surname, he was known to all and sundry as Geronimo or Zorro. His thrilling hobbies consisted of philately and collecting old postcards. He was the bodywork specialist at Haxford Fixers, and when he wasn't talking about spray-painting, or sanding down wings, he talked about his pastimes. No matter what his choice of conversation, he was perfectly capable of boring the socks off everyone, and that put him in the same class as Dennis, who could put his audience to sleep with a detailed analysis of the ignition sequence on a V-8 engine. And don't ask me to explain what that means, because I really don't know.

"So who will you take, Val?"

"Hanged if I know. I did think of Lizzie Finister, but as one of the Haxford Recorder's senior reporters, she'll probably be there anyway. What about you?"

"I can always ask Naomi," I said, "but Simon's been promoted to full DC, and there are no guarantees he'll be home to look after Bethany." Naomi was my daughter-in-law, and Bethany my granddaughter. "Failing that, I suppose I could ask Jill Bleaker from Radio Haxford, but have you ever met her?"

"I think so. Large woman, very gossipy?"

"Large is an understatement. She's gigantic, and she'll probably scoff most of the free food before anyone else can get a look in. Gossipy is an even bigger understatement. She can twist and spread stories faster than any other five people from Haxford."

"What about your next door neighbour? Mrs McQuarrie?"

"She's away with her boyfriend and his family. I can't remember exactly where but I think it's Magaluf. We haven't had a postcard yet, so must be abroad somewhere."

Val tittered. "Fancy calling Bob Emburey a

boyfriend? They're both in their eighties, aren't they? And won't Magaluf be a bit over the top for them?"

I wasn't surprised that she knew about Hazel's relationship with Robert Emburey. The local newspapers had been full of the story when I found him, and that little bit of detective work from me was what led to my now defunct Lost Friends programme on Radio Haxford.

I had to correct Val, however. "Not quite eighty, but very close. Don't let that fool you. Hazel's breakdancing days might be over, but she still likes a good time, and she'll match most of the young kids in Majorca glass for glass."

"A born again teenager?"

"I wish I had her energy. She's due back today or tonight, and after a week of living it up in the Balearics, I shouldn't have thought she'd be up for a late night at a fancy dress party."

Assuring Val that I would see her at Barncroft's Farm, I rang off and called up my address book.

I was both surprised and a little disheartened to learn just how many friends I didn't have. Plenty of acquaintances, but only two I could call friends: Detective Sergeant Mandy Hiscoe, senior officer in Haxford CID, and Kim Aspinall, assistant at the library, partner of Alden Upley, the prim and pedantic head librarian.

I tried Mandy first, but she cried off with a cynical laugh. "Some chance. With the Christmas Festival in full flow, we're on call twenty-four-seven. I'd look a right banana answering a call to a fight at the Sump Hole while dressed as Mata Hari."

31

The Sump Hole was Haxford-ese for the Engine House pub on Weaver Street, one of the roughest watering holes in the town.

"You could always ask my mother," she suggested.

"Thanks, but no thanks, Mandy. I need someone closer to my age. Besides, if you're on call, she'll be looking after Darlene, won't she?" Darlene was Mandy's year-old daughter.

"You're right, of course. What about your Stephen's wife? Melinda, is it?"

"Another one with the ability to put the sauce way, and when she gets half cut, her mouth begins freewheeling. Besides, Stephen and Melinda have taken a leaf from HazelMcQuarrie's book and gone to the Canary Islands for the week. Thanks, Mandy, and hey, if one of those big fights breaks out at Barncroft's Farm rather than at the Sump Hole, maybe I'll see you anyway."

I cut the call and rang Kim. She was my last hope. Without her it would have to be Dennis, or worse, Reggie Monk and his bad breath and BO.

Kim was cautiously interested.

"Is it vicars and tarts?" she asked when I outlined the situation.

"It certainly is not," I assured her, even though I'd never thought to check up on it.

"I might be able to make it, but the last one I got invited to at Easter was vicars and tarts and Alden went ballistic when I told him."

"He didn't fancy dressing up as a vicar?"

"The women were the vicars. The men were expected to turn up as tarts. I told him it was just a bit of fun but you know what he's like. I mean, you're funny about stuff like that, but he's a lot stricter."

Alden? Stricter than me? Not possible. I recalled seeing one or two of his adult videos during the Graveyard Poisoner case. Purely by accident, of course. It wouldn't have happened if I hadn't been so nosy, but as I'm so fond of saying, life as a private investigator is all about being nosy. As a police officer, I'd seen just about everything, but even so, such movies and videos would never find their way onto my approved viewing list.

To distract Kim, I dragged the discussion back where it belonged. "Forgetting vicars and tarts, are you interested?"

"Well, I might, but I'll have to talk it over with Alden first. What are you going as?"

"Probably Dorothy from the Wizard of Oz."

"Boring; I thought you were a big Blondie fan?"

"I am, but I wouldn't have much dressing up to do to go as Debbie Harry and most people wouldn't know who I was supposed to be."

"Yeah, but you can do better than Dorothy. If I can go, I don't know who I'll be."

It was strange listening to Kim talk this way. She had always been a confident woman, one who knew her own mind, and she had never been subdued or dominated by any man.

I made an effort to broach the matter diplomatically. "What do you mean, if you can go? Is everything all right, between you and Alden? Because I don't see how he can stop you?"

"He can't, but when I do something he doesn't agree with or doesn't like, he gets moody, and he can sit in silence for hours, days even."

"I have the same problem with Dennis, but I just leave him to it. The minute he's starving hungry, he comes round." I giggled. "It's one advantage of having a husband who can't cook." I sobered my tones slightly. "Seriously, there's no way I'd let Dennis stop me going anywhere, and you used to be more forceful when you were with whoisit... Wayne."

"Yes, but you mellow as you get older, don't you?"

"Can't say as I've noticed. But then, that's what celebrity stardom does for you." I laughed again, this time to show I was only joking. "Getting back to the do. It's organised by a mob of Larpers who meet in the woods every weekend to play witches and wizards."

"Oh, Heath Mottershaw and his pals?"

Surprise. That was my reaction. "You know about them?"

"Course I do. I work in the library, Chrissy, and he's always there. Research, he reckons, as to how things were in the sixteenth century or whenever. He even asked me to join them once over. I turned it down. I can't go anywhere without my smartphone and they're banned when those people meet up."

"How did he react to that?"

"Stuck his nose in the air. I thought, well, you can take a flying one if that's your attitude to smartphones. Come on, Chrissy, you know what it's like these days. You rely on yours."

34

"Not as much as some people. I swear some of them could do with having their phones surgically removed to stop them using the rotten things." I switched us back to the original topic. "So what about it, Kim. I don't want you to think I'm scraping the barrel, but if you say no, I'll have to take Dennis and he's a disaster when it comes to do's like this."

She laughed. "Stuff a cushion up his jumper and take him as Humpty Dumpty."

I laughed too. "I'd have to cut his hair and leave him bald."

When our chuckling settled, Kim went on more seriously, "I'm seriously not sure, Chrissy. I mean it is a bit close to Christmas."

I rang off with a feeling of disappointment. This was so unlike Kim. She was never a firebrand, but she knew her own mind and no man, not Alden Upley, not the late and largely unlamented Wayne Peason, the live-in boyfriend before Alden, would move her. And yet, now she was seeking Alden's… not exactly permission, perhaps not even his approval, but certainly his blessing before she attended a local thrash.

Dennis and I had been together for thirty years, and I'd never, repeat and stress, NEVER ask him if I could go to a, b, or c. I would tell him. Of course I would. But I would not ask. If I had something on and it clashed with another do, then fair comment, I might say, "I'll have to give this a miss, luv, because I've summat else on." It had never been a problem and naturally, it was a two way street. If I didn't have to ask Dennis, he never had to ask me… unless he was deliberately trying to wriggle out of something. It didn't happen often, but when it did, that was when I would see Dennis at his most devious.

Right now, with Val and Mandy scratched and Kim doubtful at best, I had to face the worst possible scenario: Dennis.

He landed at his usual time (getting on for seven in the evening) and half an hour later we sat down to our evening meal. Nothing flash or fancy. A couple of frozen TV dinners –I put them through the microwave first, obviously – and while we ate, I distracted him from the cars for sale columns of the Haxford Recorder.

"I'll be out for the evening on Friday."

"Oh, aye? Anywhere special?"

"The Christmas Festival Ball at the old Barncroft Farm spread. I'll be there as Radio Haxford's representative but I'll be taking a guest. Probably Kim."

It takes a lot to distract Dennis from food but that did the trick. "Kim from the library?" He waited for me to nod. "Why her? Why not me?"

"Well, Dennis, it's fancy dress."

A broad smile came to his face. "That's no problem. I can put me gangster—"

"No you can't," I interrupted. "Last time you did that, no one knew who or what you were supposed to be. If you want to come with me, you'll have to find some fancy dress, and this do is organised by a gang of black magic fanatics. How do you feel about wearing a pointed hat and waving a wand?"

"Listen, I know about this shindig, and you're

not forced to go as one of his wall locks—"

"You mean warlocks."

"Whatever. I meanersay, what else would you suggest?"

This was proving more difficult than I anticipated. "I don't know. How about a loincloth and you can go as Tarzan?"

"Forget it. I don't wanna put all the others to shame with my physique."

I actually smiled when he said that. "If you want to come, Dennis, that's fine, but I'm telling you now, I want you home here for half past four on Friday, so you'll have time to shower and shave."

That did the trick... Well, almost.

"Half past four? I don't finish work until half past six." He returned to his meal and studying the classified. A moment or two later, he abandoned them and looked me in the eye. "Here's an idea. Why don't I come home at the normal time, not bother cleaning up, and then I can go as a mechanic?"

"You are a mechanic, Dennis, and I'm not having you going to a top do like this in your work muck. If you want to come, you're home for half past four, and ready to leave at seven." I backed off. "Course, if you'd rather not bother, then I can leave the arrangements as they are."

"Yeah, but I'll miss all the free nosh, won't I?"

"In that case, it's Tarzan, or maybe the tin man from Wizard of Oz. And while we're on the subject, we need to go in town on Friday morning to choose our costumes."

I sensed that final capitulation was a matter of

minutes away.

"You're doing it again. I have to work, and I work all day on Fridays."

I held him with a steady, defiant gaze. "Your choice, Dennis, but those are the rules."

At that, he disappeared to the front room where he could admire the work Barry had done. Seconds later, he came back, took his laptop into the conservatory where he could spend the evening hoping to find episodes of *Bangers & Cash* or *Top Gear* which he might not have seen before (some hope). Cappy the Cat went with him and I filled the dishwasher before checking the same front room for Barry's progress.

Waste of time. The walls had been stripped of paper, the ceiling had been painted, and most of the woodwork was done. I found myself pining for Christmas decs which were not yet in place. Every house in the street had them but mine. Christmas trees sparkled from the windows of the Pringles at number fourteen and the Denvers at number eighteen. Even Elsie Beardley at number sixteen had put up decorations and I remembered her telling me that she was no longer interested in Christmas; not since her husband died.

It simply wasn't fair.

And as I looked through the window, a people carrier pulled up and reversed into Hazel McQuarrie's drive. She was home, her and her man, Bobby Emburey, along with Bobby's daughter and her husband.

I was tempted to rush out and greet them, but I held back. It would be too much of the 'great to see you back, what have you bought me' syndrome.

I recalled that I'd agreed to ring Jo the moment Hazel was home, and as I took out my phone, that's when the grand idea struck me. Val was a no-go, Kim was doubtful, I didn't really want Dennis showing me up, so how about...

"Hello, Jo. It's Chrissy."

"Oh hi, Chrissy. What's up? Mrs McQuarrie home, is she?"

"Just this minute. In fact, I'm watching them unload her luggage." I wasn't but Jo wouldn't know that. "Listen, while I'm on the phone, are you doing anything on Friday night?"

"Aside from sorting out Bernard's tea and then trying to find something to watch on telly. Not really. Why?"

I spent a couple of minutes explaining the situation to her, and then asked, "How would you like to come as my guest?"

"I'd love to, but are you sure Dennis won't want to go with you?"

"At this moment in time, it's finely balanced, resting on a knife edge, but I don't think he'll be that interested. Not when he has to give up half a day's work."

"Well, as long as you're sure. What will you do for a costume?"

"Haxford Costume Hire just off the High Street."

"Oh, Wilma Elmond? I went there for my witch's outfit for Halloween. She's a bit of a misery, but she's the only option in this town." A brief pause. "All right, Chrissy. Bell me once you know

39

for sure."

I cut the call. Sorted. All I had to do now was lay the pressure on Dennis until he either came to my way of thinking or backed out (with odds on the latter) and I could look forward to Friday evening.

Chapter Four

The debate between Dennis and me went on for the whole of Wednesday. At one point I suggested he go as Dracula, an idea which produced a look of horror on his face perfectly in tune with the Dracula movies.

"He's a ruddy vampire. He drinks blood. I drink Haxford Best Bitter."

"According to Reggie Monk, the prices you charge for servicing his car, it's like taking his blood."

"If that's how he feels, he can take his crummy old Ford somewhere else."

When he got home from work that evening, he finally decided that an evening of free food and drink while dressed as Napoleon Bonaparte – another of my suggestions based on the principle that he believed himself to be emperor of all he surveyed at Haxford Fixers – wasn't worth missing a morning's work and having to come home early on the same day, so he declined my kind offer. To be honest, I think he'd talked it over with Tony Wharrier and Tony persuaded him that it wasn't worth the hassle.

I hadn't heard from Kim, either, so I made a quick call and she told me that Alden had received an invite (he was, after all, the town's head librarian) and she would be going with him. From there, I rang Jo, and she confirmed that she was happy to tag along. I didn't go into the details of my persuasive efforts with my other half, but I did tell her to get a receipt for the costume hire and Radio Haxford would pay for it. Well, that's what Eric told me at the time he assumed I would be going with Dennis. Quite what he would think about Dennis hiring, say, a ballet's dancer's tutu, I didn't know and I refused to cross that bridge until I came to it.

I was out of bed early again on Thursday. I had to be to let Barry Snodgrass in and I had Adele Mottershaw to see at eleven after which I planned to nip in Haxford to collect my costume. I'd decided that despite Kim's disparaging opinion, I would go as Dorothy from the Wizard of Oz.

"Job'll be finished today, Chrissy," Barry told me as he took a cup of tea into the front room under a murderous glare from Cappy the Cat.

That reminded me I had to call at the bank to pick up his money. "Eight hundred did we say?" I asked, and he nodded.

I decided that I would add a fifty pound bonus for him, and my purse needed topping up, so I would draw nine hundred.

At half past ten I picked up my keys, and under the resentful glower of Cappy the Cat I left the house, climbed into my car and made my way into Haxford, where I doubled back along Sheffield Road and with a view of Haxford Mill half a mile to my left, I could imagine Dennis and his chums hard at it. With a shudder, I passed Springer's Builders'

Merchants, the place where I had come awfully close to meeting God during the Prater affair. I swear if the PA hadn't interfered, that brick would have smashed my head in.

Climbing the hill away from Haxford, I turned off into Keats Place, a street of 1930s-built semis, and parked outside number six.

Dennis insisted our bungalow was worth about £300,000, and I put the Mottershaws' place in the next bracket down. No bay window, flat-fronted, two bedrooms (I guessed) small front garden with a tidy lawn and flower beds, medium sized rear garden, not in a popular area (there was a large council estate less than half a mile further out on Sheffield Road).

I guessed her age at about forty-five, and she had that kind of hard-faced Haxford look about her. Black hair hanging either side of a dour face, a neat fringe above steel blue eyes and a mouth set in what I imagined was permanent disapproval. About my height, slimmer than me (there's no justice) she was dressed in a dowdy skirt and jumper and cheap, flat shoes.

She stood back to let me in and led me along the gloomy hall.

The entire place looked as if it was 'lived in' by which I mean faded, in need of some refurbishment. I thought perhaps I should give her Barry Snodgrass's number but I'd already decided I didn't like her and she hadn't said or done anything yet.

As I passed along the hall, I noticed one or two photographs on the wall away from the staircase. One was of her and (I assumed) her husband, the man I was to interview a few days hence. About the same age as Adele, he must been about six feet tall judging from her height. His dark hair was getting thin on top, and there was something insincere about the way he was smiling into the camera, as if he had been ordered to smile. Like his wife he was dressed slightly dowdily, as if he couldn't be bothered smartening himself up. Or maybe he was like Dennis, a working man, used to overalls, and to him, his casual trousers and wrinkled shirt would be smart.

Next to that picture was another, and this time it was Heath alone. He was wearing a long, bright blue gown decorated with astrological symbols, and sported a tall pointed hat, also covered in symbols which I couldn't quite make out. He also wore a long, grey wig and matching beard, and carried a foot-long, knobbly stick, presumably his wand.

We came to the kitchen, where she waved me to a cheap, laminate-topped table while she switched the kettle on.

"You'll have tea?"

I put a question mark after it but she phrased it more like an order than a query.

I agreed and she joined me. She took out cigarettes, lit one and blew the smoke at a ceiling fan. Neither I nor Dennis smoked, and even if we did, we wouldn't while we had guests. And what she thought the fan would do, I don't know. Spread the toxins evenly round the room? It certainly couldn't get rid of it the way our extractor would.

We passed a few minutes with small talk. Did I find her place easily enough? Was I getting ready for Christmas? Was life as a private eye busy? As she talked there was an edge about her voice, and a significant lack of interest in my responses.

Eventually the kettle boiled and she made tea, splashing a generous helping of full cream milk in. She stirred, picked up the beakers, handed one to me and sat opposite. She lit a second cigarette, and I moved us on to business.

"So your problem, Mrs Mottershaw?"

"Adele, please."

"Very well. Your problem?"

"My husband. Heath. He's thieving."

"Hmm. I thought you said you'd been robbed, and I did say it's a job for the police."

Blowing another cloud of smoke at the ceiling, she faced me again, and shook her head. "And I told you, I can't go to the filth with it."

"I'm struggling here, Adele," I told her. "If you've been robbed, you need to report it, if only so your insurance will cover it. If your husband is stealing and you don't take him to the law, it could get worse."

"I know all that, but you don't know the whole story yet." Another drag on the cigarette, another fine stream of smoke blown at the ceiling mounted fan before she delivered the *coup de grace*. "I'm the one he's stealing from."

Silence followed, interrupted only by the soft whirr of the ceiling fan.

I took a gulp of tea. It was awful, but I was so gobsmacked by her last announcement that I hardly noticed.

"I… I'm sorry, but I don't understand. How is it

45

possible for a husband to steal from his wife? Unless you're separated or divorced or something. I mean, if my Dennis went through my purse and took twenty or thirty pounds I'd notice and there'd be a bit of argument, but I wouldn't accuse him of stealing it. The same applies if I rifle his wallet."

"He's not taking money. Like you and your old man, what's mine is his and what's his is mine."

"Tell me something. Are you always this skilled at confusing people?"

"Not long on patience, are you? Is it all a put on when you're playing the agony aunt?"

I'd had enough of her biting tone. "No, it's not. I pride myself on being patient and willing to listen and help where I can. But most people tend to speak plain English, or plain Haxford. It would help if you got to the nitty gritty and told me exactly what's going through your mind."

She was as skilled as Eric Reitman when it came to not listening, or giving the appearance of not listening. But in fact, my insistence struck home.

More smoke hit the fan (not a double entendre) and she went into her tale. "My grandma died when I was a kid. She left her engagement and wedding rings to my old ma who snuffed it about five years ago, and those rings came to me. They disappeared last weekend. We haven't had a burglary nor nothing, I didn't take them so he must have."

"Have you confronted him?"

"Do fish wee in the sea?"

(Note: she didn't actually say it like that, but her basic, working class vernacular is far too vulgar for a sensitive soul like me to include in this text.)

46

"He denied it and accused me of misplacing them. Hell, I haven't touched them in god knows how long. No. He took them and he's either pawned them or sold them outright. All I need you to do is track them down."

If it sounded a simple proposition, a little thought soon dissuaded me. "It won't be easy, and it could be expensive."

"I can afford you."

"Yes, well, the first thing you need to know is that I can only track them down if they've gone to a pawnbroker or a jeweller who takes second hand goods, and even then it could take some doing. If he's sold them privately, it'll be almost impossible for me to find them."

Adele took a final drag on her cigarette and stubbed it. Concentrating on me, she shook her head and promptly disagreed with her previous assertion. "He hasn't sold them off. He wouldn't dare. He's pawned them. Listen, missus, I know him. I should do. We're coming up to twenty years wed. His business is suffering with this cost of living thing. He needs cash and the easy way to raise it is to hock off my gran's rings."

This did not make a lot of sense. "What kind of business is he in?"

My question produced a cynical smile. The first I'd seen from her and I was surprised her face didn't crack under the strain. "You mean you don't know? You should. He knows your old man really well." When my face betrayed total mystification, she announced, "Heath is a second hand car dealer. He has a place off Huddersfield Road. Motty's

47

Motors."

"Oh. Right." I had passed it hundreds of times. Even so, her claim still didn't make sense. "Well, surely, the second hand value of a couple of rings won't be much use if he has cash flow problems."

"The band of gold might not be worth much more than, say, fifty quid, and you'd be pushing your luck to get that off a pawnbroker. The engagement ring is different. It's a diamond cluster around a large, central sapphire, and I've had it valued – for insurance purposes, you understand – at a bit over two grand. Not sure what he'd get from a pawnbroker but it'd help him meet the site rent and business rates, if only for another month, and if he can sell a couple of motors in the meantime, he can redeem them."

"In that case, you could check the pawnbrokers yourself."

"Haven't time. I work three or four days a week as a one to one teacher. In any case, you private eyes have contacts like a dog has fleas, don't you? All I need you to do is find the damn things, maybe buy them off whoever has them and then bring them to me. I'll make sure you get the money back, plus whatever you charge for your work."

I had to stop and think about this. There were not many pawnbrokers in Haxford. Perhaps half a dozen, and three of those were in the town centre. She could get round those in the space of a morning. So why was she willing to pay?

It's not often that Dennis could teach me a lesson, but this was one of those exceptions which proved the rule. 'When a customer asks, don't quibble, just do it and bill him.' That was Dennis all over; a highly skilled auto-engineer but a total mercenary when it came to business.

"The thing is, Adele, you need to understand that I charge thirty pounds an hour and a job like this is quite labour intensive. It could cost you anything up to three or four hundred by the time I've tracked these rings down, and if they are with a pawnbroker, you'll have the cost of getting them back."

"I told you, I can afford you. Beside, when you prove it to me, I'll take the cost out of his wallet... and his hide." She fumed for a moment. "By the time I'm done with him, he'll be the only forty-something, wannabe wizard who can sing soprano."

She was getting mad, so as a distraction, I asked, "Eric Reitman at Radio Haxford told me about this LARP thing your husband's involved in. What part do you play? Are you the good witch or something?" In truth I suspected a fair number of years had gone by since anyone would describe her as good. She was moodier than Cappy the Cat.

It backfired. Rather than calming down, she became more incensed. "Me? I don't have nothing to do with those clowns other than playing hell when I want a good night out and their larping gets in the way. It's all Heath." She dug out another cigarette and made a show of lighting it. "You know what he calls himself? Theah. It's spelled T-H-E-A-H."

I frowned. "Theah?"

"It works like this." She sat slightly forward, leaned on the table and treated me to lungful of

49

passive smoke. "It's all based on stuff like Harry Potter, but Heath wanted to come up with names that were original. Took him ages to sort it all out, and when he did, it boiled down to simple idiocy. Theah is Heath spelled backwards, with the a and e and the t and h switched round to make it easier to pronounce. He did the same with the rest of the gang. Roger Trippet is now the Dark Lord Regor. Alf Dalby is Derfla, Bill Killey is now Yellik, and Donald James is Lanod. The top witch is a woman called Katya Watkins, and she's named Aytak, spelled A-Y-T-A-K." She gave out a harsh, barking laugh, followed by a bout of coughing as the cigarette smoke got to her. "Brainless dorks," she said when she could speak again. "The lot of 'em. Running round Hattersley Woods like a gang of schoolkids every weekend."

I recalled that I had reacted in a similar manner when Eric first told me what the Haxford Larpers did with their spare time. On the other hand...

"Katya Watkins? Am I right in thinking she's a checkout supervisor at CutCost?"

"The same. And she's every bit the witch and bitch there as she is in Hattersley Woods every weekend."

Time to change the angle of attack. "You're happy to put up with Heath's play-acting, are you?"

"It gets him out from under my feet," she replied. "Except, like I said, when I fancy a night on the tiles. Anyroad up, never mind him and his gormless gang. What are you gonna do about my rings?"

I was still more than a little suspicious of her

real motive but I could see no way out of it, so I stood by Dennis's advice. "All right, if you really want me to try and track them down, I will, but it won't be cheap. First I'll need a photograph of the rings, or ones that are similar, so I know exactly what I'm looking for. I don't suppose you have one."

"As a matter of fact I have. Let me Bluetooth it to you."

A few moments later, I had the photograph on my phone. "Only the engagement ring?" I asked.

"There was never any point photographing the wedding ring. Nowt special about it. Just a plain band of gold. Not even an engraving on the inside."

I studied the image. Like she said, this was an expensive piece of brass and glass. What I knew about the value of jewellery could probably be written on a postage stamp, but I knew this was pricey. A gold ring, a cluster of small diamonds set around a large central sapphire. I think Dennis would need to put in a year's worth of overtime to buy me anything like this.

"All right, Adele. Leave it with me and I'll get back to you when I have some news."

Chapter Five

Ten minutes later, I climbed into my car, did a six point turn, and drove out of Keats Place and back down Sheffield Road towards Haxford, my mind still churning the twists and turns of the last hour, still harbouring suspicion.

Marital disharmony tended to be the most straightforward of cases. Most of the time it was infidelity or the suspicion of same, and it was easy to put myself in the client's shoes. How would I react if Dennis was unfaithful to me? How would he react if the situation was the other way round? Not that it ever would be on either side of the equation. Dennis did deceive me, but it was only on the amount he spent cossetting his precious Morris Marina, and I did keep things from him, such as what it cost to kit me out for the thrash at Christmas Manor the previous year.

People often told me that I had a neo-Victorian attitude to adultery. Did I? Well, if so, I wasn't about to loosen the reins just to please others.

I digress. That was the usual run-of-the-mill marital case. Adele Mottershaw's problem was a different and as far as I was concerned, unprecedented proposition. In this day and age of fifty-fifty partnerships, especially when it came to divorce, how was it possible for a husband to steal from his wife or vice versa? If he really had done what she insisted he had, then he was deceiving her just like Dennis did with me, like I did with him. More extreme for sure, but not theft in the accepted sense of the word.

And how come she hadn't been able to sort it out herself? She was the kind of hard-faced harridan who looked as if she kept a set of brass knuckles in her handbag. The kind you wouldn't like to meet down a dark alley after you'd overcharged her for cigarettes. And to judge from her threats, if her husband wasn't worried about her now, would be when (if) I tracked down the missing jewellery.

Right now, however, I had other business to deal with. I needed a costume for Friday night, and a receipt to make sure Radio Haxford paid me for the hire. No point reminding Jo to do that if I forgot it for myself, was there?

Parking behind the market hall, I made my way down to the High Street and then onto West Street. It wasn't as grand as it sounds. It didn't even lead west. It was roughly north-south. A short and narrow thoroughfare sporting a couple of pawnbrokers (yes I checked them and saw no sign of Adele Mottershaw's ring) one or two charity shops, a few offices, and Haxford Costume Hire.

I'd been here in the past (for the Millennium do I mentioned earlier) and what never occurred to me was that Wilma Elmond, the proprietor, might just be related to Adele. Why would it, considering I'd only just met Adele? In truth, I didn't know that Haxford Costume Hire was owned by someone named Wilma Elmond until I saw the little sign under the top of the entrance. You know the kind of thing I mean. A narrow strip painted chocolate brown with white lettering which you normally find under pub doors reading something like, 'Joe Bloggs licensed to sell... etc. etc. etc.' This one simply said, 'Haxford Costume Hire, prop: Wilma Elmond'. It didn't mention any licence for alcoholic drinks. Even then, I never made the connection and I should have done because she looked a lot like Adele Mottershaw and she had the same sour attitude.

She was behind the glass-topped counter, and as I approached, I noticed that she offered a range of costume jewellery. Whether it was for sale or hire I didn't know, but I did know that Adele's ring was not on display.

I greeted her with a smile. "I've been invited to the Christmas Festival Ball at the old Barncroft place tomorrow night," I announced, "And I'm thinking of Dorothy from the Wizard of Oz."

She gave a Haxford tut and shook her head. "I only have the one Dorothy and it's out." The voice was laced in gravel which went perfectly with her appearance.

That took the smile off my face. "It won't be back in time for me to hire it?"

She shrugged. "Shouldn't think so. The woman who's hired it is going to the Christmas Festival Ball, same as you, so unless she changes her mind this side of dinner time, or snuffs it or summat..." She trailed off, unwilling to expend energy on stating the obvious.

54

Just what I didn't need. "All right. What else can you recommend?"

She looked me up and down as if assessing what I should look like. "Plenty of cowgirl costumes, but they might be a bit tight on you."

Thank you very much. If I was looking for veiled insults, I could have gone down to Haxford Fixers and talked to Dennis.

While I was trying to think up a suitable rejoinder, she went on. "How about Madame de Pompadour? She was doing the business for Louis the something or other."

"Louis the XV," I told her. Thoughts of Kim's tarts and vicars crossed my mind. "And she died of tuberculosis, so I'll pass if you don't mind."

"All right. How about Aphrodite, Greek goddess of love and horizontal PT? I can do you the toga, the wig, and a golden apple to go with it." She waited, but my face must have telegraphed my doubts to her. "What? No go?"

"Fact is, I'm representing Radio Haxford. I'm Christine Capper. You might not have heard of me—"

"I know who you are. I'll listen to your agony aunt spot now and again, and as far as I'm aware, you're interviewing my brother-in-law next Monday."

"Your brother-in-law?"

"Heath Mottershaw. He's one of the idiot Larpers and he's married to my sister, Adele."

That's when everything came together in my head. "Oh. Sorry. I didn't realise. You look a bit like her, too."

55

"Not many people make the connection. We haven't had nowt to do with one another for years, so it's not something I broadcast." The scowl returned to her cragged features. "Now, are you interested in Aphrodite?"

"Could I have a look, try it on?"

She agreed and led the way back across the shop to a rail holding a multitude of costumes. As we passed an open door, I glanced into a rear room littered with garments and other bits and pieces, such as Perseus's plastic sword and a fake head of Medusa complete with snakes. Thrown to one corner, I could see Darth Vader's mask, and there was a mannequin nearby wearing the almost non-existent costume of Princess Leia when she was a slave to Jabba the whatchamacallit... shed, I mean Hutt, and next to that was grandma's nightie and wolf mask from Little Red Riding Hood.

After rifling through the rail, Wilma took down the toga, handed it to me, and then led me to the opposite corner and a small changing cubicle.

And by small, I mean miniscule. I barely had room to strip down to my undies, and I'm sure that my lower legs were visible under the door. You can judge how small the cubicle was because when I pulled the toga on, I was stretching my arms out and both of them collided with the walls of the cubicle.

This tiny box was possessed of a three-quarter length mirror, which granted me the opportunity to study the effect. Quite frankly, it hung on me like an overlarge piece of sacking. It was designed to be off the shoulder, but this was so large, if I wasn't careful, it would be off my arm, and displaying more of my, ahem, attributes than I cared to show.

I dredged the depths of my memory, recalling images I'd seen of Aphrodite. In many cases, she wore nothing at all, and on some occasions when she wore a toga, it was lowered to her waist, displaying those bits most of us would be reluctant to display in public. I had no desire to emulate her.

On the other hand, the toga was a good idea but it depended on Wilma Elmond. As a full body garment it would hide most of me, and from that angle, it would be quite respectable, even erudite, for a radio personality to wear at a fancy dress do. Always assuming Wilma had a smaller size.

Hiding behind the door, I half opened it and poked my head out. "It's a bit big."

Her eyebrows rose. "That's a surprise."

I swear, if I had many more oblique comments on my minimal weight gain, I would go to the ball as Perseus, and I'd be carrying that head of Medusa, aka Wilma Elmond, in my hand.

"Do you have a smaller size?" I asked.

"I do, but it might be too small."

That was it. That was just about as much as I was willing to take. I slid my brain into overdrive, determined to think up some smart remark that would pay her back. Something like, 'well at least I don't have to sidestep to avoid falling through the slots in the kerbside drain covers.'

Why is it that some people can come up with them on the spot? Do they spend hours rehearsing them, and then wait for the appropriate opportunity to spit them out? It took me so long to compose and rehearse a catty comment that by the time I was ready to deliver it, she had crossed to the clothing rail again, rifled through it, and was now on her way back with a replacement toga.

The second one was a little tight around the hip, but it stayed on the shoulder, not off it, and the remainder, all the way down to my ankles, was sufficiently flouncy to hide whatever sins I preferred to keep to myself. And don't ask what those sins are. I harboured a suspicion that they were linked to chocolate digestive biscuits and Warrington's irresistible cream cakes. I think it was an allergy. I was allergic to not eating them.

Satisfied that I would look all right, I took off the toga and proceeded to dress. The sleeves of my light, white top had got tangled up when I took it off and as I put it back on, I had to force my left arm through it, as a result of which, I manged to punch the mirror. It didn't break but the whole cubicle shook like jelly in a hurricane and for a moment I thought it was going to collapse, which would have been a bit unfortunate because I hadn't put my jeans back on. As you will no doubt realise, I'm quite shy about such things, and I had no desire to flash next week's laundry to such passers-by who might glance through the shop window.

It held and when I was dressed again and came back out, I said, "I'll take that," and followed up with, "You know, you could do with a bigger cubicle."

"Not normally a problem for my customers," she said and refused to elucidate.

I now reckoned the score at three or four-nil to her and while I was turning over possible comebacks and/or common assault, she spoke again.

"You want the rug that goes with it?"

I frowned. "Rug?" I had visions of a comfy, fireside sheepskin which Cappy the Cat could dig his claws into. Well, it would make a change from him digging them into me. However, I couldn't ever recall seeing artists' impressions of Aphrodite carrying her own front rug, so…

"Yeah. You know. A rug. A syrup." She reached under the counter and came back with a fiery red wig. "A hairpiece."

I twigged. Syrup – syrup of figs – was more cockney slang than Yorkshire, but rug was common enough in Haxford. "I don't think so," I said eventually. "I spend a fortune at Sonya's every month."

"Sonya's?" This time, the scathing tones were tainted with incredulity. "Wouldn't it be cheaper to go to Silver's butchers in the market, get them to lop it off with a meat knife?"

By now, her slights on my weight and my hairstylist had ignited my anger and I could feel it increasing. "Are you from Haxford?"

"Born and bred."

"Only you don't seem too happy with the place or the traders." I could have added 'or me' but I didn't.

"I'm not. Face it, Mrs Radio Haxford, the place is a dump."

"Hmm. Not sure I agree with you there."

"Well, you wouldn't, would you? I mean you get paid to paint the pretty side of life in this hell hole." She reached under the counter again and this time came out with a golden apple. "This'll cost you twenty all up, twenty-five if you're paying with plastic."

"No choice, I'm afraid," I said as I took out my credit card. I flashed it over the card reader, put it back in my purse and picked up my golden apple... my golden, *plastic* apple, as I realised when I felt the weight. As plastic as my credit card.

Wilma handed me a receipt, and then produced a large form which she began to fill in at various places. "You have to sign here to say you accept responsibility for any loss of or damage to the equipment."

I bristled. "Shouldn't you have done that before you asked me to pay?"

"Slipped my mind." She turned the form to face me. "Sign and date and name in block letters."

I scanned it quickly. It was the standard sort of insurance proposition and the only quibble I had was her version of Aphrodite, which she spelled, *Aprodhietey*. I nevertheless signed and dated it and spelled out my name before handing it back, and she passed me a carrier bag containing the toga and golden apple.

As I got ready to leave, I said, "Interestingly enough your sister's just hired me."

"Gran's missing engagement ring?" She snorted. "I've been hearing about it. Silly cow even rang me, accused me of nicking it. As if. I haven't been to her place since I can't remember when."

Time, I decided to get out of there. "Well, thank you, Mrs Elmond. I'll return the costume Saturday or Monday at the latest, dependent on how much I have to drink tomorrow night."

I dropped the Aphrodite clothing and accoutrements (i.e. the golden plastic apple) in my car, and that's when it occurred to me that the entire ensemble had no pockets. Where would I keep my essential baggage, my purse, my phone, lipstick, face powder, tissues and the million and one other items I wouldn't normally leave home without? Right there and then, it was all in my handbag, which was about the size of a CutCost carrier, and weighed almost as much as my granddaughter, but I didn't fancy carting that about at a formal do like the Christmas Festival Ball.

The answer was obvious. Cut down the essentials to the absolutely cannot leave home without, and use a small bag, and I had a range of small clutch bags which would do, but I wasn't exactly sure that any of them would match the off white (or not properly laundered or just plain old) costume I'd hired.

You're no doubt thinking that this was just an excuse to buy a new bag. Nothing could be further from my mind but as it turned out, five minutes later I was perusing the offerings at Hattie's Handbags on the outdoor market where I had a lovely chat with old Hattie, a lady who had been a near permanent fixture on the market for something like forty years. I had my eye on a neat little purse for a tenner, but never let it be said that Hattie didn't know how to sell. She faffed about with all the chains securing the bags to the stall, stopping people actually stealing the bags, and showed me a smashing little clutch bag in off white with a silver (all right, highly polished stainless steel) chain for less than twenty pounds.

Then, as I came away, I happened to spot the shoe stall next door, and I remembered I would need Greek sandals to finish off my ensemble. Aphrodite was, after all a Greek goddess.

I'd seen these things on the web at prices of anything up to £200. Pass. But I did get a pair in faux leather (plastic again) for a tenner.

Thus armed, I headed for the car, debating whether I had time for a quick toasted teacake and tea at Terry's Tea Bar, but right out of the blue, the problem of Heath Mottershaw's (alleged) thievery came back to me with a vengeance.

What hadn't occurred to me, at least until I unlocked my trusty, rusty Renault Clio, was the problem I had created for myself in the shape of Radio Haxford and the Christine Capper Interview.

Four days hence, I was scheduled to interview Heath Mottershaw for the station. How would he feel when I showed up having exposed him as a deceitful husband? He was unlikely to be charitable and I could foresee him refusing to talk to me. Even if I left the confrontation until after the interview, he would still go to town on Radio Haxford and me. I didn't know the man but as a used car dealer it was practically certain that he was active on social media. Worse, he was sure to have an account with the Haxford Recorder and he wouldn't be slow to remove it unless Ian Noiland ran a piece running me and the station down. And I knew Noiland well. Old (dating) friends we might be, but he would willingly sacrifice me before letting an advertising account go.

As usual, it was a dilemma entirely of my own making. Adele's case interested me despite my suspicions, and I let that, plus the chance of making a few pounds – all right, a few hundred pounds – blind me to the complexities.

What to do, what to do? Dig up some background information, that's what, and hadn't Adele told me that Heath knew my husband? With luck, Dennis might have enough dirt on Heath or even Adele, to let me force them into toeing the line.

I settled behind the wheel, started the car and set off. Next stop Haxford Mill and the Haxford Fixers workshop.

And then I had a rethink.

Adele had mentioned Katya Watkins as one of the Larpers. I knew her… slightly. Mind, so did most of Haxford, and I don't necessarily mean knew her in the biblical sense. She was a renowned snapper (and slapper for all I knew). Would she know anything about a missing sapphire ring?

There was only one way to find out.

Chapter Six

I would never claim that CutCost was my favourite port of call. In truth, it was a necessary evil because it was the only large supermarket in the town. Yes, we had branches of all the nationals, but they were small, minimarkets. CutCost was a Haxford institution and even though they'd gone national, they maintained a giant, "buy everything here" branch on Huddersfield Road.

I called once a week for our buying in, and I'd been going there so long, I knew where everything was. I could get round the place in less than half an hour... unless Dennis was with me. At those times, he spent so much time whinging about the cost and arguing with me, that the chore took twice as long.

I also knew most of the staff, and they knew me, which didn't do me any favours at the checkout, but it did help pass the time with amiable people.

That didn't apply to everyone working there. As Adele hinted, and as I already knew, you couldn't tag Katya Watkins with the 'amiable' label.

A good ten years younger than me, she was quite tall for a woman. Somewhere around five foot ten, with a slim body, a shower of blonde hair and blue eyes that aimed daggers wherever they looked. It's tempting to say she was attractive when she smiled but it would be pure guesswork because I'd never seen her smile. She was a good match for Adele and Wilma in that she could cut diamonds with the sharp edge in her voice. Not particularly loud but certainly vicious.

I had shopping to deal with and it was a toss-up whether she'd be on duty, but as luck would have it, she was the supervisor, lording it over the scan-and-shop equipment. You know the kind of thing I mean. You scan your purchase as you go round the shop and it adds your bill up for you. Dennis insisted that it merely prolonged the palpitations which, he was sure, would lead to a coronary one day, but for me, it meant no queuing at the checkout when you were done. You just aimed the ray gun at the specialised, non-attended checkouts and it did the rest for you.

"Except pay the ruddy bill," Dennis would often observe.

I did the shopping (without a list) and made my way to the checkout where a member of staff had to confirm that I was old enough to buy paracetamol tablets – quite flattering in an absurd sort of way – then paid the bill and finally collared Katya as she was putting the scanners back in their charging sockets.

"I believe you're a member of Haxford Larpers," I said.

"What business is that of yours?"

You see what I mean about snappy?

"Well, I'm interviewing Heath next Monday, and—"

"Good for you. Now would you mind clearing

65

off so I can get on with my work?"

I knew it wouldn't take long to go downhill but I'd anticipated it taking slightly longer than this. "Didn't anyone ever teach you any manners?"

"Not when I'm dealing with nosy mares like you. I know who you are. Now bugger off."

"Did you know Adele Mottershaw's lost her grandma's engagement ring?"

"How many times do —"

"She's hired me to look into it, and she suspects you might have it, courtesy of Heath. If I find—"

"Say that again and I'll flatten you."

"And lose your cushy little job? I don't think so. And before you think about taking me on, lady, let me remind you, I used to be a cop. I'm perfectly capable of handling people like you." I turned, ready to leave, and glanced over my shoulder. "I'll be watching you."

As I was ready to walk away, the assistant manager, Aidan Compton came hurrying to us. "Is there some problem, Mrs Capper, Katya?"

"Nothing I can't handle, Mr Compton," Katya declared.

"A simple exchange, Aidan," I said. "You know, you really should train your staff a little better. It's not good for customer relations when one of them tells a customer to bug... go away in no uncertain terms."

He looked uncertainly from me to Katya and back again. "Katya—"

"She was hassling me, Mr Compton. Summat about an engagement ring, and she accused me of nicking it."

"I did nothing of the kind. I was merely repeating something someone else said to me."

"Yes, well, do you think we can keep it down? Mrs Capper is one of our most loyal customers, Katya." Aidan turned to me. "On the other hand, if you need to speak to Katya on matters which are of no concern to CutCost, it would be better if you did so when she's not working. Regarding Katya's rudeness would you like to make a formal complaint?"

I declined with a sour glance at the woman. "No. But bear in mind, Katya, I may need to speak to you again."

And with that, I turned my back and walked out. Feeling quite pleased but not a little irritated, I climbed into my car and started the engine. Next port of call, Haxford Fixers.

Haxford Mill was a part of Haxford's history which dated back to the Industrial Revolution when Squire Barncroft decided to bring the village into the 18th century and mechanise the gathering and processing of wool, a project which turned Haxford from a small village, its hovels straggling the banks of the sluggish River Hax, into a small and (eventually) thriving town.

When the last of the Barncrofts died out, the mill became the property of the local authority who, unable to demolish it, turned it into a business centre housing all kinds of entrepreneurs on its three floors, including the two units rented by Haxford Fixers.

They were on the ground floor, along the river wall side (I use the word 'river' because that's how the Hax was described on maps. In truth it's more like a trickle). Dennis's place was easy to find. In fact, you could spot it from the air when aircraft making for Manchester or Leeds and Bradford flew low enough. From the moment they opened the doors about ten years back Dennis and his three partners were working non-stop, six, sometimes seven, days a week.

Dennis and his close friend Tony Wharrier (Val's husband) were the senior partners. Lester Grimes and latterly Greg Vetch were the juniors but it had to be said the Greg was fast overtaking Lester purely by virtue of his work rate. Greg could match Dennis and Tony job for job, day for day. Lester couldn't, and if truth be told, didn't want to.

They were in mufti when I walked into the workshop, winding down to the afternoon tea break. Dennis was tinkering, applying spanners to some complicated bit of a car on his workbench, Greg was in the pit working under an ageing Ford Escort and Lester was sat at his bench in the background, a tumble dryer open, it's electrical innards exposed while Lester sat back, hands clasped behind his head while he listened to Radio Haxford. Tony was noticeable by his absence but in fact, he was where he always was, where he liked to be; in the paint/body shop next door where I could hear him pottering about.

Almost without exception, Lester would be the first to notice me when I called at the workshop, but for once, it was Dennis who registered my presence first.

"Hey up, lass. What are you doing here? I

thought you'd be getting your stuff together ready for the big shindig tomorrow night." He checked the wall clock above his bench and grinned. "I meanersay, the time it takes you to get ready I'd have thought you're behind schedule already."

"Take a little advice, Dennis. If you're planning on becoming a comedian, stick to mending cars."

That was the prompt for Lester to turn round and deliver a salacious grin. "It's kissable Chrissy. What are you looking for, darling? A rave with a right old raver?"

I gave him a false smile. "I might if you slipped into something more comfortable, Lester."

Aware that I was leading him on, he frowned. "Something more comfortable? Like what?"

"Lancashire."

Even Dennis laughed. "Terrible thing to say to a Yorkshireman. Anyway, what was it you wanted? Nowt wrong with the car, is there?"

"No, love, the car's fine. I'm chasing information as always. I need to know what you know about Heath Mottershaw."

The smile disappeared from my old man's face. "Motty? What about him?"

I scored myself a point for having guessed that Dennis and his pals would know something. "His wife said you knew him and the minute I learned he was a used car salesman, I guessed you would."

"Yeah, well, see, whenever he sells a motor he sends it to us for a full service and valet. Haven't heard nowt from him for a week or three now."

"She also told me he was struggling. People don't have the money for new cars."

"New nothing. They're second-hand. Aye, and he don't half sell some rubbish. You should know. You're driving round in one of his wrecks."

I bristled. "You leave my little Renault alone."

"He took it as a part exchange from some mug, and we gave him two ton for it, and as I told you, we intended doing it up and flogging it. We'd have got five for it, I'm sure. But we never got the chance, did we? You wanted it in exchange for that crummy Fiat."

After the assault on Dennis the previous year, the wealthy McCruddens, who were in many ways the catalyst for that attack, appeased their conscience by handing us a power wheelchair and a nearly new Fiat Diablo. Once Dennis was fully fit, the Diablo was too big for us, so I did a straight swap with Haxford Fixers: the Diablo in exchange for my nippy little Renault Clio

Determined to challenge him, I demanded, "And how much did you get for the Diablo when you sold it?"

Dennis didn't answer. He suddenly found the engine bits he was working on to be the focus of supreme interest.

Instead, Greg Vetch replied from beneath the car he was working on. "Nine and a half, Chrissy."

I smiled triumph at my lesser half.

"I wish you'd learn to shut your trap, Herriot," Dennis grumbled before focussing on me. "So what were you doing talking to Motty's missus?"

"Business, Dennis. Confidential business. You know, like you selling a Fiat Diablo for almost a thousand pounds which you never told me about."

"I didn't sell it. Haxford Fixers did. Anyway, you reckon you were talking business to Adele Mottershaw? What you really mean is you're poking your nose in where it doesn't concern you... again."

"But it does concern me. She hired me. She's paying me. And anyway, in case you've forgotten, I'm interviewing Heath Mottershaw for Radio Haxford next Monday. About his involvement in the Haxford Larpers."

"A bunch of bananas," Greg said crawling out from the pit. "Carrying on like a mob of schoolkids every weekend. Like extras from a failed Harry Potter movie. Crap excuse for a bit of how's your father in Hattersley Woods if you want my opinion."

Dennis grinned and Lester cackled. I could feel my ears colouring but Greg's assertion diverted my attention sufficiently to avoid a full scale blush. Not that I had anything to blush over. Dennis and I had been together for the better end of three decades and I could honestly say that when it came to visiting Hattersley Woods, we never indulged in anything heavier than snogging. Until we got our own place, we always had Dennis's car for anything more adventurous.

From the back of the workshop, Lester found it impossible to avoid commenting. "A bit of horizontal exercise in the long grass, eh? Hey up, do you think they'd take me on? I could be the wandering magical minstrel of the woods."

I had my comeback ready. "Trouble is, Lester, they won't serve Haxford Best Bitter."

71

He tutted. "Always a snag, ain't there?"

Ignoring him, I concentrated on Greg and Dennis. "Naughty goings on? Is that just scuttlebutt?"

Dennis pursed his lips and shook his head. "More than a grain of truth in it. Especially while that Roger Trippet's playing with 'em."

Greg backed him up. "And if you wanna know about Trippet, ask Sandra up in the Snacky. She's sampled his supposed assets… I think."

I had to admit, if only to myself, that it would be entirely in keeping with Sandra Limpkin's behaviour. About fifty with a couple of longish relationships behind her, she was a classic example of growing old disgracefully and not giving a fig for what other people thought of her, and to be honest, I liked her.

"In that case," I said, "I'll nip up to the Snacky and have a word with her."

I turned to leave, but Dennis stopped me.

"Just a minute. What's this business Adele's hired you for?"

"I told you, Dennis, it's confidential." I gave him a sly smile. "Let's just say that Heath Mottershaw might not be the little angel you think he is."

My other half snorted. "Adele didn't need to hire you to find that out. All she had to do was ask me. Remember, I've seen some of the lemons he sells to his punters."

"I know you have, love, but I'll bet he didn't steal any of them from his wife."

Feeling quite proud of myself and the way I'd

left them puzzled but none the wiser, I made my way out of the workshop, ran to the front of the building where I took the lift up to the third floor and Sandra's Snacky.

The cafeteria took up most of the third floor and was one of the focal points of Haxford Mill. Most of the businesses located in the building called for their food and drinks, and a good number of the customers of those businesses also called for refreshment. I have to say that Dennis and his partners were Sandra's biggest supporters. They either went for breakfast or had it delivered to the workshop, they took lunch there and their afternoon snacks. According to Dennis, Sandra did the finest full English breakfast in Yorkshire, which made it all the more surprising that he would come home every evening starving hungry. Correction; it might be a surprise to other people, but not to me. Remember the old adage of eating like a horse? Well, my husband could out-eat any two nags under starter's orders.

Short (about my height) blonde-ish, stocky, slightly overweight, Sandra was also loud. She was what I would term WYSIWYG. What you see is what you get. She called a spade a fizzing shovel and she didn't care who heard.

When I got there, she and her daughter, Ulrika, and her brainless son, Tommy, were in the process of cleaning down, leaving just enough cups and plates available for the afternoon customers, but she was happy enough to break off and join me for a cup of tea at one of the tables closest to the service counter.

"Heath Mottershaw and his Larpers?" she asked with a level of incredulity that could be heard all over the mill. "What are you doing mixing with those barmpots?"

"Business, Sandra. And I'm sorry, but it's confidential. I was just talking to Dennis, to see what he could tell me about Heath, and Greg Vetch hinted that you knew... well, not so much Mottershaw as Roger Trippet."

She laughed. "I know Roger, all right. And he knows me. He came looking for a favour, and laid a line of chat on me, promising to take me to heaven if I could do what he asked. I told him where to stick it."

Given her reputation for entertaining different men, that admission came as a bit of a surprise.

"You're going a bit too fast for me here, Sandra. What exactly did Trippet want?"

"It wasn't him at first. It was Motty. You know he runs this wizards and witches thing every weekend?" She waited for me to nod. "Well he wanted to sign me up as the good witch Cookham. That way, I could go to Hattersley Woods every weekend, and make meals for them, waving my magic wand over a portable stove. It was never really on, Chrissy, because when I asked him how much it would pay me, he said, and I quote, nothing. Zip, zilch, zero. So naturally I told him where he could shove his wand and his portable stove. A couple of days later, Trippet called here, and tried to sweet talk me into his king-size bed, if I agreed to turn out with the rest of the nutjobs every weekend. I told him where he could go, and he could take his king-size bed with him. I mean, come on, you're a businesswoman. When do you work for nothing?"

The question made me feel a little downcast. "You'd be surprised at the number of people who want a private eye but they don't want to pay for one. I never got paid for that business with Georgie Tibbett. Come to that, I didn't get paid for cracking Anita Stocker's problems. The only income I can rely on is Radio Haxford, but they only poppy up every quarter." I forced a lighter tone upon myself. "But I understand what you mean. I have to interview Mottershaw for Radio Haxford next Monday, and I'm just seeking a little background on him." I chuckled. "Radio Haxford are a bit hot on interviewers not overstepping the mark. You told me about Roger Trippet. Is Heath Mottershaw of the same inclination?"

Sandra shrugged. "Search me. He never tried his luck. Mind, there's this little tramp that hangs about with them. Katya Watkins. She has a bit of a reputation, but it's hearsay. I can tell you that Trippet is – or was, married, and so is Motty, and I don't know if you've met Adele—"

"We've met," I interrupted. "The same goes for Katya."

"Yes, well, in that case, you'll know that if Heath was playing away, Katya would be favourite, and Adele wouldn't leave much for the pathologist, and what she did leave would look more like a woman than a man."

The imagery produced by her words sent another shudder through me. "Thanks, Sandra. I'll take it all on... Oh, just out of pure nosiness, do you

75

know how well Mottershaw's business is doing?"

She had to think for a moment, carefully calculated her words. "Put it this way. If my steak and kidney puddings were doing as well as his car sales, I'd switch to meat and tater pies."

Chapter Seven

When I finally got home, it was to find the work on the front room finished and Barry Snodgrass tidying up. He invited me to check it out, and I fell instantly in love with him... I mean it (he wasn't really my type).

Whenever Dennis had practical, refurbishment work to do around the house, he always did a classy job, but this was absolute perfection.

"Just a little matter of settling the bill, Chrissy," he told me, and a shock ran through me.

I blushed. I'd been so busy flitting about here and there that I forgot to call at the bank. "I...er... oh dear."

"You haven't got it, have you?"

By now, my face must have been glowing like a traffic light. "I'm sorry, Barry. I was so busy—"

He cut me off as he looked down his nose at me. "I do get this with other people. People taking the mick and who can't afford the bill, but I expected better of you and Cappy."

His veiled accusation stung. "I do have it, Barry. I was supposed to go the bank and draw it for you. I forgot." I checked my watch. Four-thirty. "I think the bank closes at five."

"Woollen district?" When I nodded he shook

his head. "It closes in about two minutes."

"Oh dear, oh dear, oh dear. I can't write you a cheque either because we don't have chequebooks these days."

"So I have to come back tomorrow? It'll cost you another—"

This time I cut him off. "Wait. Let me see if Dennis has that kind of money in the petty cash at Haxford Fixers." I took out my smartphone and rang my other half.

Impatient as ever, he listened, and then started losing it. "You were supposed to get the money for him."

"I forgot. Don't you forget things?"

"Never?"

"Yes you do. You forgot our anniversary last year. You had to go rushing to Breakfast to Bedtime to get a card before I got out of bed that morning. Yes, and even then you got the wrong damn card, didn't you?"

"I mean I don't forget important stuff."

"And our anniversary isn't important? Well, thank you for nothing, Dennis. Now, have you got enough in petty cash to pay Barry?"

"No. We only leave a coupla hundred notes on the premises for emergencies, but give me five minutes and I'll see if Sandra can help us out. How much do we need?"

"Eight fifty."

"I thought it was eight even."

"The way we're messing him about, he deserves extra."

"I'll bell you back."

Dennis cut the call and I smiled obsequiously at Barry. "I'm sorry about this. I really am. Dennis is trying to get the money together for you. Would you like a cup of tea while we wait?"

He chuckled and shook his head. "All right, Chrissy. I can see you're trying and I'd like to get off home. What say I call back tomorrow? Give you time to get to the bank."

I hadn't planned on going anywhere on Friday, but whether it was to pay Barry or get the money for Dennis to pay back Sandra Limpkin, I no longer had a choice. "Tell you what. You know Terry's Tea Bar in the market hall? Could you meet me there about quarter past ten and I promise I'll have the cash for you."

"I'll be there."

"Thanks, Barry, and I really am sorry for this."

As he gathered his gear together and left, Dennis rang back. "Sandra says she can lend us the eight, and we have the odd fifty here."

"It doesn't matter, Dennis. I've sorted it out. I'll meet Barry in the market tomorrow morning after I've been to the bank."

"Tsk. You're messing me about, you are."

"Well, that's what husbands are for, isn't it? At least that's what you always say. Just forget I ever spoke, Dennis, the way you usually do, and I'll see you when you get home."

I wasn't really angry with Dennis. I was more annoyed with myself. Organisation was one of my strong points (so I would insist) but I had been anything but organised today and there was no excuse for it. What better way to ameliorate my

79

irritation than to take it out on Dennis?

Alone at last, I decided it was time to try on the toga and make sure I was up to scratch for the following night, but before I could, the phone rang. Kim.

"Just checking, Chrissy. How are you getting to Barncroft's Farm tomorrow night? Driving?"

"I wasn't planning to. I don't know how much I'll be drinking, and let's face it, a do like this, I'll need a snifter or two."

"Well, how about we pick you up? Me and Alden?"

"It's a bit out of your way, isn't it? And won't Alden be drinking?"

"Strictly lemonade and tonic water." She giggled. "He'll be on lemonade cos he'll be driving, and I'll be drinking the tonic water, topped up with a bit of mother's ruin. We can pick you up and drop you off later. Honest, it's no sweat."

"All right then. About sevenish?"

"We'll be there."

"One way, Kim. I'll get Dennis to pick me up when I've had enough."

"Of the party or of the drink?"

"Either. Both."

That was another issue sorted. If only I could have been that well organised earlier, or had someone to get me that well organised.

Once again I picked up the toga, but as I turned for the bedroom (it was the only room where we had a large enough mirror for me to properly assess my appearance) the rotten phone rang again. Jo this time.

"Just checking that everything is ticketyboo for tomorrow night, Chrissy."

"It will be if I ever get around to trying on my costume." I sighed at my own annoyance. "Sorry, Jo. I've had one of those days. Have you got your costume?"

"Yes. I'm going as Cleopatra." She gave a naughty chuckle. "It doesn't show too much skin."

Thank the lord for that, I thought, I didn't say it. Instead, I asked, "Did you sort out Hazel's care arrangements?"

"Monday, Wednesday, Friday every week," she replied. "Starting on the Wednesday of the first week of the New Year."

"Oh, good. Well, don't forget when you've done with her, call for a chat and a cuppa. I'm free those days."

"Count on it. Now how are you getting to Barncroft's Farm tomorrow night?"

"I've just arranged it with Kim Aspinall. She'll pick me up and I'll get Dennis to come for me when I'm ready for home."

"We can drop you. Bernard and me."

"No, don't worry. It won't be a problem for Dennis. It's miles out of your way. Listen, Jo, I'll have to ring off or I'll never get this fancy dress sorted. I'll see you tomorrow."

I killed the call and at last made my way to the bedroom where I stripped down to my undies, and drew the toga over my head.

Not bad, I thought as I checked in the full length, wardrobe mirror. At a second glance, I noticed that when I was moving, the gown shuffled around my shoulders and my bra straps showed. No problem. I'd wear a strapless bar. A few minutes later, suitably attired, I checked again. Perfection, I decided. Only it wasn't.

Like any genuine woman, I need to see what I looked like from behind, so I nipped to the bathroom, borrowed Dennis's free-standing shaving mirror, returned to the bedroom and stood with my back to the wardrobe. The deep V of the toga's back left my strapless bra showing. Worse, it was showing the clasp. It would only need one drunken idiot to go for that, and I could be sagging all over the place.

I dressed and made my way back to the kitchen where I sat with a cup of tea mulling over possible solutions. At a pinch, I could always get the sewing machine out and stitch the plunging back up a little, but what would Wilma Elmond have to say about that? Radio Haxford were happy to pick up the bill for hire, but would they pay for 'damages'? Unlikely. And no matter how carefully I unpicked the stitching before returning it, Wilma would be sure to notice.

I was still thinking about possible options when Dennis got home. We took our evening meal together and while I chewed on a defrosted hotpot, I also chewed on this problem.

Dennis was saying something about the cars he was working on, but I wasn't listening and he wasn't slow to complain. "You know, there's times when I might as well be invisible for all the notice you take of me."

Bing! No, I'm not talking about Microsoft's

search engine. It was that word, invisible. That was the answer. An invisible bra.

After tea and listening to Dennis's trials and tribulations with a 'clapped out Hyundai', not one word of which I understood, I had a quick look online and decided they were too expensive. I would buy one in Haxford on Friday morning.

***

Never let it be said I'm not a woman of my word. I was at the head of the queue when the bank opened at 9:30 on Friday morning, and ten minutes later, I came out with £900 in my purse, enough to pay off Barry and leave me with sufficient for bits and pieces.

With time to spare, I did a little window shopping at Haxford's few lingerie outlets, and learned that the online prices were not alone in their outrageousness. As I joined Barry at Terry's Tea Bar, I realised I would have to go back to CutCost to look for my invisible bra, and after the previous day's head to head with Katya Watkins and to a lesser degree, Aidan Compton, it was not a pleasant prospect.

When I handed him the money, Barry counted it and then proved himself more of a gentleman than Dennis could ever be when he handed back the extra fifty.

"I could see it were a genuine error, Chrissy."

I pushed it back across the table. "And you did such a good job, Barry, that I'd decided to pay you the extra anyway. Now don't argue. Take it. Dennis can afford it."

He laughed. "Does he know about it?"

"No, but let's keep it our secret, eh?"

I passed a pleasant twenty minutes with Barry before he went on his way, then treated myself to another cup of Terry's excellent tea before making my way back to the car, and heading for CutCost. I was not looking for groceries, instead I would be wandering round the clothing department on the upper floor (CutCost literally did sell everything) and with luck, I wouldn't even see Katya Watkins, never mind meet her.

Well, we all know my luck don't we? Bad.

It took me a while to find the invisible bras, but I managed to pick one up for less than ten pounds. It was theoretically skin coloured but it looked more like red to me, which made me question how that could be described as 'invisible'. Under the toga, yes, but suppose I wanted to wear it with a thin, white T-shirt? It would be visible all over Fuengirola. (Come on. I'd never be able to wear a thin, white T-shirt in Haxford.) Nevertheless, I paid for it and made my way to the exit. As I reached ground floor and headed for the doors, I bumped into Katya.

She glowered. "You got me hauled over the coals."

"Well, I just hope they were glowing red hot."

"You're walking a tightrope with my temper."

"And you're pushing me to the edge. I didn't come here yesterday looking for a fight. I wanted to ask you a few simple questions concerning the Haxford Larpers. You were the one who got out of the pram first." From the corner of my eye I could see Aidan Compton making his way hurriedly towards us. "And right now, I have more to do than stand here arguing with you."

She seethed. "It must be awful to get to your age and learn that you're nothing more than a nosy cow."

"Don't worry about it," I advised her. "The way you annoy people, you probably won't live to be my age."

For a moment I thought she was going to lose it altogether, but Aidan arrived. "Ladies. Please—"

I interrupted to reassure him. "It's all right, Aidan. Ms Watkins was just apologising for yesterday's misunderstanding. And if you'll excuse me, I have a busy day ahead of me."

"That'll be the bloody day when I apologise to the likes of you."

I had already turned away, preparing to leave, but her remark sparked a flash of temper. I turned back. "You don't know when you're well off. I was about to let it all go, but since you seem incapable of controlling your mouth, maybe I should start asking serious questions about Adele Mottershaw's missing ring."

"You can get—"

"That's enough." It was Aidan interrupting her this time. "Katya, you have been warned once." Now he rounded on me. "You are one of our most loyal customers, Mrs Capper, but if you persist in harassing my staff, I may have to consider barring you from the store."

"Teach her some manners, Aidan," I declared,

and this time, I did march out.

I had some shopping of the Christmas variety to pick up (choccies, sweeties, other goodies, a few decs, etc.) and normally I would have dealt with it in CutCost but the spat with Katya had annoyed me to the point where I wouldn't give them the pleasure... or the profit.

Even so, I wasn't feeling too pleased with myself when I left the store. I should have ignored her when she first opened her mouth, but backing down under that kind of verbal aggression was not the Haxford way. It wasn't mine either.

As I climbed into my car, I turned that argument almost on its head. Yes, I should have ignored her, but her attitude did beg the question, why was she so het up about my presence. It was tempting to think she really did have Adele's ring, but that would be incredibly difficult to prove. On the other hand, I never mentioned the ring until after she began hassling me on Thursday afternoon. In fact, as I thought about it, she was ready to do battle from the moment we met. Indeed, she behaved almost as if she was expecting me on Thursday.

How could that be, I asked myself as I drove along Huddersfield Road on my way back into town.

And then I remembered my suspicions regarding Adele Mottershaw's true motives, and how I had reflected on the manner in which most marital cases involved adultery.

There were, I decided as I parked on the market pay and display, two possibilities. Adele suspected Heath of infidelity and after I left the previous day, she rang Katya warning her that she had an expert on the job (me, in case you're struggling to work out who the expert is). The second possibility was that Adele rang her husband and told him the same story, letting him know that she was onto him and intended nailing him to the wall for some serious alimony when she got to the truth.

One of the underlying principles of engaging a private eye was that you tell the truth. What was the point in laying out money for such assistance and then lying to him/her? And yet, I had the feeling the Adele Mottershaw was lying through her (false?) teeth.

Never let it be said that Christine Capper was afraid of challenging her clients.

I picked up the Christmas bits and pieces I needed, then drove home. I say bits and pieces, it was well past one o'clock by the time I pulled into Bracken Close and switched the engine off.

Letting myself in, I put the kettle on and took out my smartphone, ready to ring Adele, but Cappy the Cat demanded some attention. I let him out and while he was busy in the Timmins's garden, I put a feed down for him. When he came back (he wasn't gone long because he never is when the weather's rough) I settled in the conservatory with my tea and rang Adele.

She answered on the second ring, almost as if she had been sat by the phone waiting for it to ring.

"Mrs Mottershaw? It's Chris—"

"News?" she interrupted. She really was one of the rudest women I'd ever met.

"Yes, and none of it is good. I checked the local

pawnbrokers and there's no sign of your mother's engagement ring."

"Grandmother's," she corrected me.

"Yes, well, no one is offering it in their window, but if Heath took it and pawned it. They wouldn't put it up for sale, would they? You yourself said he would be looking to redeem it."

"Damn. And you didn't hassle these pawnbrokers?"

"No, I didn't. They wouldn't talk to me anyway. That kind of transaction is confidential and they'd only go into details with the police. Even then, the law would need a court order."

"Damn, damn, damn. I'm wasting my money with you, aren't I? Sort out your final—"

I cut her off. "Not so fast." I allowed a momentary pause to ensure she was listening. "Have you spoken to Katya Watkins about hiring me?"

"I don't speak to Katya Watkins at all other than to tell her to get out of my sight. Why?"

"I've had two arguments with her in the last twenty-four hours is why, and the first time it was almost as if she was expecting me."

"Nothing to do with me. Send me your bill and I'll make sure you're paid."

"Fine, but just to be clear, if I turn up any more information, by accident or design, you'll owe me more."

"No problem." And with that, she cut the call.

Chapter Eight

When I visited Haxford Fixers on Thursday, Dennis made a fly remark about the amount of time it takes me to get ready. No way would it take me a day and half to get ready for an evening out, but I must admit that he had a point. It does take me a long time, but that's because I'm a perfectionist (that's my excuse and I'm sticking to it).

After the brief, curt and rude exchange with Adele I decided I needed a dose of normality, so I set up the Christmas tree and spent some time hanging baubles and other trimmings on it. As always, I was short of tinsel and I made a mental note to pick some up when I was in Haxford next.

Then I looked at the clock and it was gone three. How could the simple job of arranging a few trinkets on a fake tree take so long?

Not to worry I still had time in hand, so I set about placing other Christmassy stuff under the TV set. I knew that Dennis would complain that they interfered with the remote because he moaned about it every December, and no matter how careful I was to keep the Santas and robins and reindeer away from the receiver on the TV set, he still struggled to channel hop for the whole month. I think it was because he was too lazy to aim the handset accurately, but hey, what do I know? Nothing according to my other half.

I checked the clock again and almost had a heart attack. Half past four? How was that possible?

Time, I decided as I put away my box of Christmas decs, to start getting ready.

I began with a shower and a half hour titivating my hair before putting on several layers of makeup.

It was only then that I unpacked the invisible bra and realised it was backless and strapless. Why hadn't I noticed that when I checked online? I think Dennis must have distracted me. I couldn't work out what would hold it in place? Was I supposed to tack the cups on with Sellotape, or maybe pin them to… Well I couldn't think where I would pin them.

Then I read the packaging and learned that it was a stick on affair. I wish I'd read it properly before I parted with the better part of £8 for it.

I was none too happy about gluing this thing to my bosom. I mean, when it came to removing it, would it rip away one of my nipples? It was also described as 'just the thing for every babe'. Since when could I be described as a BABE? Aside from finding the term cringeworthy and offensive, I hadn't been a babe for thirty years or more.

Still, it said it was skin friendly, and with the thought that it was probably the kind of thing my daughter-in-law, Naomi, must have in her wardrobe, I came to the conclusion that I was a good deal more out of touch than I ever imagined.

It was too late to worry about it, so I put it on and then drew the toga on over it. Did everything live up to expectations? Not really. It was more like living down to un-expectations. The bra simply made my bubbles sag a little further than normal, and I had a horrible vision of myself in twenty or thirty years' time: an old woman with her vital curves on a downward spiral. No way could I stand that, so I threw everything off, chucked the stick-on flopper stopper to the carpet, and put on a tried and tested, reliable support instead, then pinned the back V of the toga with a (I hoped) a discreet safety pin and put it back on.

Once fully attired, temper cooling, I stood before the wardrobe mirror and asked myself did I look like Aphrodite? Not really, but by the time everyone had availed themselves of the free drinks, who would care? She was a goddess, a classically beautiful woman. I was a Haxford housewife, good looking (so I insist) in my own special way, but hardly a classic beauty... except to Dennis, and that was usually when he was either drunk or he wanted something... and no, I don't mean he wanted what you think he wanted. I mean when he wanted some pricey widget – such as an eight-track and cartridges – for his precious Morris Marina.

The reflection which greeted me was more like Christine Capper than Aphrodite but I could probably excuse myself on the grounds that the only Greek I knew was *'efcharisto'* which means 'thank you'. I learned it when we were in Cyprus a few years back.

Carrying the (plastic) golden apple did nothing to boost my appearance either. In fact, it was a darn nuisance. The toga had no pockets I could put the thing in. Well, it wouldn't would it? In most of the pictures I'd seen of Aphrodite she wasn't wearing the toga never mind the pockets. In fact she wasn't wearing anything at all, and it did cause me to wonder where she stowed the golden apple when she wasn't seen carrying it.

The rotten thing wouldn't fit in my new clutch bag either, but I have to say that said bag, thrown casually about my neck, went well with the toga.

Which was more than could be said about my wristwatch. I mean, how many Greek goddesses do you see sporting a £50, gold-plated Sekonda? Dennis bought it me for our 25th wedding anniversary. Yes, I know that's the *silver* wedding celebration, but I always preferred gold. And it's not that Dennis knew he bought it for me. I bought it on his credit card. He just signed the gift tag when I told him to. Even then, he spelled anniversary as 'avinursery'.

I was digressing into fond memories, and I didn't have the time. Literally, if I took the watch off, and I would have to if it wasn't to look out of place.

Another memory struck me. We're very traditional in Haxford, and whenever someone reached the age of 21, you bought them a gold watch. We did so for Ingrid and she was very grateful, but I noticed something in her expression when she opened it, almost as if it was not what she really wanted. It was Kim from the library who clued me up.

"No one wears wristwatches these days, Chrissy."

"Which accounts for the way most of them

92

don't know what day it is never mind what time it is."

"No, no, no. They have the time don't they? On smartphones."

With that in mind, I took the watch off. Never let it be said that Christine Capper didn't keep up with trends.

And talking of trends, I stared resentfully at the invisible bra now cluttering up the carpet. Eight pounds down the drain, and I would have to bury the flipping thing in the dustbins just in case Dennis spotted it. Not that he would realise its purpose. He'd probably imagine it to be a pair of upmarket kneepads for when he had to kneel on the workshop's concrete floor, but there would still be some kind of inquest, if only because he'd never be able to work out why they were joined in the centre by a slender thread of fabric.

The one concession I made to the 21st century was earrings. No way would I go out without them for fear of some idiot trying to jam cocktail sticks in the holes in my ear. I dug out an old pair of gold stirrup hoops, and hung those in place. I'd had them a good number of years, and it was a bit risky because the spring clasps were getting a bit worn. Whenever I wore them I invariably lost one or the other. Still, they matched the plastic apple, with the possible exception that they were genuine gold, not paint.

The next problem was footwear. In all the pictures I'd seen, Aphrodite wasn't wearing shoes. As I've pointed out so often, it was entirely in keeping with the rest of her. Even in a crowd of men and women she was still in the altogether. But if anyone thought for one moment that I would walk round the old Barncroft's Farm with nothing on my feet, they had another think coming. The Greek sandals were absolutely spot on, but when I checked through the windows, it was threatening rain. Wellies would be more suitable, albeit unrepresentative. No way was I going to trail out there in weather like that wearing nothing but a few strands of plastic attached to a sole and held together by even more strands of plastic. In the end, I chose an old pair of taupe-coloured wedges after ensuring that the hem of the toga covered them. If it was too muddy, the toga would get mucked up, not the taupe uppers, and in that event, Wilma Elmond could deal with the laundry. She would anyway, wouldn't she? I mean, surely she couldn't just send a costume out after someone had worn it without washing it. Could she?

It was as I came to the conclusion that she probably would, that I checked the clock again and I was mortified to learn it was getting on for half past six. It shouldn't really have come as a surprise. Sunset was ten to four, and when I finished faffing with my Christmas decs, it was dark.

Right then I still hadn't heard from Kim and I needed to know where she was up to. I snatched up the phone and was about to dial her when my mobile rang. Dennis.

"What do you want?" I demanded. "I'm in a hurry."

"I were just ringing to check whether you'd be there when I get home, only I'm ready for leaving work now."

"The way things are going, I'll still be here when you've finished your dinner."

"Oh good. It'll save me—"

"I was being sarcastic, Dennis. I'll leave one of those CutCost frozen breakfasts for you. Make sure you read the instructions before you put it in the microwave."

I could almost hear him shrugging. "Whatever. If your new wallpaper gets burned, you're to blame for not being there."

"How can you burn the new wallpaper? The microwave's in the kitchen."

"I mean the new kitchen wallpaper."

Barry had redecorated the kitchen during the summer, but even Dennis couldn't make a mess of a microwaved dinner. Could he? I took him to task. "Many more comments like that and I'll feed your dinner to Cappy the Cat and leave you to starve. Now would you mind clearing off so I can speak to Kim?"

He rang off and now that I had the smartphone in my hand, I used it to call Kim.

"Just wondered what time to expect you," I announced when she answered.

"Oh. Right. I'm ready. I'm already in my cozzy and I'm only waiting for Alden."

"So tell me about your costume?"

She giggled again. "Oh, no. You can wait and see when we get there. We'll pick you up in about twenty minutes."

While I waited, I rang Dennis, only to get his voicemail, and I knew what the situation was. He

95

was driving and he'd forgotten to put the phone on hands free. Either that or he wasn't talking to me because I wouldn't cook his dinner.

I was in the front room when Alden's car parked across our drive, and Dennis's Marina trolled up behind it. As I stepped out of the house, Dennis was at Alden's window haranguing him about blocking our drive off.

At least, that's what I thought but when I joined them I realised that my old man and Alden were in a sympathetic, 'me too' debate, and I don't mean they'd been sexually harassed. I mean they were comparing lifestyles partnered to women who were determined to do their own (innocent) thing for a fun evening.

Breaking into their debate, I said, "Alden and Kim have been invited, Dennis, so they've kindly offered me a lift. I don't want to impose too much on them so you can come and pick me up later."

"Yeah. Right enough. About tennish?"

"Try no earlier than midnight."

"Yeah, but I have to be up for work tomorrow."

"I'm sure you'll cope." I gave him my sweetest, meaningless smile. "I'll ring you when I'm ready to come home."

Leaving Dennis glowering at me, I climbed into the back seat of Alden's Vauxhall and settled in alongside Kim. I noticed that Alden was dressed as aWW2 solider, and an officer at that; well, he would be wouldn't he? Can't have the chief librarian dressed as a square bashing squaddie.

He pulled forward of our gate to let Dennis in, then reversed into the drive and pulled out towards the end of Bracken Close where he turned left into Moor Road for Haxford and all points north and west.

"It's good of you to pick me up like this, Alden," I said.

I can be extraordinarily adept at flannel when I want. The truth was Alden probably had no choice. Kim would have insisted the way I had just done with Dennis.

"I don't mind, Mrs Capper," he said as we cruised down the hill to town. "At least you'll arrive safely and I'm sure your husband will ensure you get home equally safely."

And I was just as sure as him, but I didn't say so. "You know, Alden, we've known each other long enough for you to call me Christine."

"We are acquaintances, madam. Hardly close friends and I think that would be impolite at the very least."

Kim nudged me and gave the tiniest shake of her head, hinting that I should let it drop, so I deliberately focussed on her. "Who's he supposed to be?" I whispered.

"Field Marshal Montgomery."

I nodded and looked her over. She was wearing a heavy, fake fur coat to keep out the chill. So was I, but unlike hers, anyone could see the hem of my toga. All I could see beneath her coat was her bare calves and feet in plain black, sensible shoes.

"So, are you going to show me your fancy dress?" I asked.

With a wide grin and staring at the back of her partner's head, she was determined to wind him up, and she said, "I'm going as Princess Leia."

I was horrified. Hadn't I seen that costume in Wilma Elmond's shop that very morning? It amounted to nothing more than a fancy, bronze finish bikini which left precious little to the imagination.

She smiled at me and then again at the back of Alden's head. Like an idiot I rose to the bait.

"How do you feel about that, Alden?"

"It's an improvement on the last absurd idea Kim put to me. Vicars and ladies of the night indeed."

Now I was gobsmacked. How on earth could the near nudity of a bikini be better than...? "But she must be all but naked under her coat," I protested.

The car wobbled and I think it was my fault. Opening my trap like that must have touched an Alden nerve.

"I beg your pardon."

I looked from the back of his head to Kim to the back of his head to Kim and she couldn't hold back any longer. She burst out laughing.

"You are so easy to dupe, Chrissy." She giggled again and then threw open her coat to reveal not the slave bikini but Leia's white tunic, only knee-length, considerably shorter than it was in the movies, but readily recognisable.

"But I thought—"

Kim cut me off. "You know what thought did. Do you seriously think I'd go to a do at Barncroft's Farm in a bikini at this time of year? It's cold enough in this damn thing." She fingered the tunic as the 'damn thing' in question. "Anyway, who are you supposed to be? Julius Caesar's mistress?"

That caused the car to wobble again.

Ignoring Alden's narrow-mindedness, I corrected Kim. "I'm Aphrodite, the Greek goddess of love," I replied and dug into my coat pocket. "And look. I even have a golden apple... It's plastic," I explained as she took it from me.

"Better keep it out of Dennis's way when you get home, else he'll eat it."

I didn't reply. I couldn't think of anything to say to such an accurate assessment.

**

Barncroft's Farm was a ramshackle shed of a place constructed of old, local stone. It had stood there for over nigh on three hundred years, and it looked it. The local historical society had applied for listed status on a number of occasions and been kicked back every time. Better buildings from the same era had been demolished and Haxford Borough Council didn't even bother approaching the government department responsible for listing such sites.

Looking at the place you couldn't blame the council. It would have been akin to granting listed status to the local rubbish dump. As matters stood, it was scheduled for demolition and the whisper had it that some big movie star was looking to build there. Haxford had a reputation for Chinese whispers, but this one was easy to dismiss. California, Haxford was not. It wasn't even Pinewood. Therefore, no movie megastar would consider living anywhere near the town. I think the closest we came was some young, wannabe actor who'd had a walk on part in Coronation Street twenty years ago and was now employed as a shelf filler at CutCost.

Naturally, I knew all this when Eric first mentioned the Christmas Ball, and I had wondered quite where they were going to hold the soirée.

The answer was obvious the moment Alden pulled into the car park twenty minutes after leaving our house.

During the annual Wool Fair, they erected a huge marquee (aka the beer tent) and the Haxford Larpers, or the council (I wasn't sure which) had gone to the same trouble now. Not quite as large as that used for the Wool Fair, but big enough to accommodate the invited guests. To take care of their – ahem – other needs, there was a line of portaloos discreetly set at the rear and out of general sight, close to the side wall of the farmhouse.

We were a few minutes early, but even from the outside, it was clear the place was crowded. As we neared the entrance where two uniformed security officers were checking the invites, I hung back.

"Summat wrong, Chrissy?" Kim asked.

"I have to wait for Jo. She's my guest and they won't let her in if I'm not there. You and Alden go ahead. I'll catch up with you somewhere inside."

I had no idea what kind of car Bernard Petheridge drove, and I didn't know what he looked like, so all I could do was keep a look out for Jo dressed as Cleopatra.

It was nippy standing there, too, especially dressed in an off the shoulder toga, and my coat tried its best but it could feel the chill getting to me. I chose to take a peek inside the marquee but before I could, the security bods stopped me.

"Sorry, missus. Invitation only."

I dug into my bag. "I have an invitation. Christine Capper, Radio Haxford. Or do you think I dress like this all the time?" They stood back but I declined. "I'm waiting for my guest and it's a bit taters out here." Taters is another Yorkshireism for cold.

"Stand just inside then, luv. You'll be able to see your guest coming."

It made sense, so I stepped in just to the left of the entrance where I could look out and back at the car park.

But of course, the scene inside was much too compelling for a nosy biddy like me, so I took a good look.

It was quite crowded. I could see a range of Santas, several fairies, at least three wizards, two witches, and an assortment of other costumes, including Alden already making his presence known as Field Marshal Montgomery.

A violin quartet were playing on the small stage, in front of which people were dancing. behind the band was a tower clock and at first, I thought it was just a prop, but as I watched, the hands moved from 7:29 to 7:30.

It was a puzzle. Why did they need a clock?

"Search me," the taller security man said when I asked. "He'll know." He pointed to a tall man in a bright blue cloak and pointed hat. I recognised him instantly as Heath Mottershaw. "Motty," the security man confirmed. "He organised it all."

I was tempted to go over and ask him, but at that moment, a Kia Soul pulled into the car park and Jo got out. I waved to her, and she came towards me, a smile beaming across her lips.

"You made it then?" I asked as we hugged.

"Couldn't wait."

I authorised her with the security men and we moved into the marquee proper.

Chapter Nine

Once inside, a young man took our coats and gave us a couple of tickets so we could reclaim them later. They looked like raffle tickets to me and as I followed Jo into the crowded area, I hoped no one would raffle off my coat. It had a few years on its back, true, and I wouldn't miss it too much, but it was a cold night and Dennis's ageing Marina was not the warmest car on the road.

My new friend looked fabulous as Cleopatra. True, she was a good ten or twenty years older than the queen of the Nile was alleged to be when she clocked out, but Jo's black hair, hanging down either side of her face, was a natural for the part, and the ornate gold (coloured) chains strung about her head matched the stylised images of Cleo which were so familiar. Her toga was a bit chancier than mine. Totally off shoulder at both sides, gold braiding around the deep V-neck and capped sleeves, it bared a serious amount of cleavage. A lot more than I would dare, especially on a freezing night in Haxford. I'd be cautious about showing that much if I was in Benidorm or Playa de Las Américas never mind West Yorkshire,.

"You look great," I told her trying to keep the edge of envy out of my voice.

"You don't look so bad yourself, Chrissy. Shall we mingle?"

"Keep tabs on me," I said as we made for the drinks table. "I'm here in an official capacity so I need to lay off the sauce."

Jo sighed. "I envy you. Fame and fortune on the radio."

I laughed as I picked up what I hoped was a glass of champagne. "More like notoriety. And you can forget the fortune bit."

Heath Mottershaw, tall, slender, looking a total idiot, bowed in welcome.

"Good evening, my dear lady. May the beneficence of Theah the Mighty bestow glorious fortune upon you both?"

You can guess why I said he looked like a total idiot, can't you? As well as the photograph I'd seen in the Mottershaw's hallway, his fake name told me who he was, and putting aside his wife's opinion from Thursday, the notion of his idiocy, was enhanced by his dress; long, flowing robes in bright, electric blue, decked with astrological and magic signs, his head topped with a tall, pointed hat, also covered in occult symbols, and a fake beard stuck to his sideburns and chin.

I smiled and said nothing. Jo was more honest. "Your whiskers are coming undone, Mr Mottershaw," she said, and pointed to his left ear where his fake beard was coming away.

He gave us a second smile, then turned away to attend to his fancy dress.

Jo wandered off seeking more interesting company, and I looked around... seeking more interesting company.

The place was absolutely packed with many famous, historical figures. I counted at least two more Aphrodites, or should I say two more women wearing togas, but to be honest, neither of them had a golden apple. There was one more Princess Leia, and she was partnered by someone geared up as Han Solo. There were so many wizards and witches and Santas that it was difficult to count them. I saw Napoleon Bonaparte sipping a glass of champagne and talking to Sir Lancelot who was struggling to drink champagne because the pointed helmet of his armour got in the way. Alongside them, a young man wearing the red shirt and white shorts of George Best (his name was on the back of the shirt) was yattering with a woman who I assumed was Mata Hari. For sure, she was showing as much skin as all the images I'd seen of Mata Hari, but to be fair, she could just as easily have been Fanny Hill in operational mode.

I picked up another glass of what I hoped would be champagne, and ambled slowly around the room, ignoring Abraham Lincoln passing the time with a Roman centurion, and Florence Nightingale chatting with a slimmed down version of the Incredible Hulk, and I do mean slimmed down. He was thin as a rake, in place of a six pack, he had a pancake, and if he had any muscle anywhere, it certainly wasn't on his arms or his chest. As I passed them by, I wondered how he would get rid of all that green makeup on his face and bared chest. Well, I assumed it was makeup. If it was paint, he'd be in for a sore old time scrubbing it off. I also wondered how he would cope with the December cold. Perhaps his parents were picking him up later, and maybe they'd bring an overcoat with them.

To one side of the marquee, couples were dancing (and I mean proper, arm in arm dancing, not jiggling about the floor) to the music put out by the violin foursome. They were playing... well I don't know what they were playing because I couldn't hear properly over the general hubbub of conversation, the clink of glasses, and occasional, half-drunken cackle. What puzzled me most was the band's dress. They appeared to be clad in Edwardian evening dress. So who were they supposed to be?

"The musicians from the Titanic," a voice in my right ear told me. "Remember. And the band played on."

I smiled up at the man stood alongside me. "Before my time, I'm afraid, and I never did see the film."

He stood head and shoulders taller than me, and his height was exaggerated by a pointed hat, black this time, and covered in different occult signs to the ones I'd seen on Heath Mottershaw's garb. It matched his robe, which was also black, also decked with what I fondly imagined were black magic signs, including several skulls, and to complete the crass ensemble, he had hung a medallion on a chain round his neck. He was obviously wearing a wig, flowing, grey hair, sweeping down over his shoulders, augmented by a tiny beard attached to his chin.

"Are you one of the Larpers?"

He bowed his head seriously, solemnly. "I am the Dark Lord Regor."

"Ah. Real name Roger Trippet."

He gave me a smile which was just as evil as his attire suggested. "Someone has been talking out of turn, have they?"

I offered my hand and he shook it. "Christine Capper. Radio Haxford."

"Oh. Of course. You're interviewing Theah – I mean Heath about our fun and games, aren't you?"

I nodded. "On Monday, as it happens, but it would be nice to get some background on the Haxford Larpers. For example, what do you do for a living in real life?"

"I'm a, er, benefits advisor."

"A worthy profession considering the complexities of claiming benefits," I said. "And I know this is a social do, but how long have you been involved with Haxford Larpers?"

"Ever since my good friend Heath came up with the idea." He looked me up and down and deliberately changed the subject as if I was getting too close to questions he might not want to answer. "May I say, you look delightful? I assume you're some kind of Roman serving wench?"

I vowed I would get him for that. "Aphrodite," I replied and brandished my plastic apple. "The Greek goddess of love."

"And temptation," he noted. "Curious how the humble apple has become synonymous with sin, isn't it? A Greek goddess carrying a golden apple, Eve tempting Adam in the Garden of Eden with an apple. Tell me, Mrs Capper, is such fruit really an aphrodisiac?"

"I haven't a clue, and at my time of life, it's not something I tend to think about. How about you, Mr Trippet? Is LARP really nothing more than an excuse for, let's say, adult games?"

The look on his face told me that honour had been satisfied. Roman serving wench indeed.

"Nothing of the kind. We take our games quite seriously. Or would you prefer that we were obsessed with work... like your husband?"

I noted his knowledge of my other half. "Does Dennis service your car?"

He nodded. "For many years. My wife's too." That smile came back to his lips. "As Larpers, we are dedicated to our role play. To us, it is real life in a different dimension. Now do you see why I found your suggestion of LARP as an excuse for – what did you call them – adult games so objectionable?"

Pull the other one. The thought had crossed my mind and it was based on nothing other than the leer in his eyes. And Sandra Limpkin's say-so. Frankly, I hadn't a clue what he was trying to say, but I didn't want to admit it, so I agreed instead. "Oh, yes, I do. Please excuse me, but I must circulate." I scored the brief interlude at 2-1 to me, and having decided that I didn't like him, didn't trust him, I felt the least I could do was retire gracefully from the conversation.

I wandered on, weaving in and out of little cliques, passed a couple of Draculas chatting with Wolfman – probably comparing notes on the paucity of human targets during the year's lousy summer – and spotted Kim talking to a woman at the food table. A redhead done up as Elizabeth I, she held her left hand forward, palm down, showing off her rings to my friend, and Kim looked about as interested as she would be if the woman were showing off her corns and bunions.

I thought I'd better rescue Kim, but before I could get there, I bumped into Val Wharrier.

She too was wearing a toga, but she looked more like a lady wrestler than any Greek or Roman goddess. I always said there was a lot of her. Not that she was unlovely, and certainly not fat, but just big.

"Good do," she greeted me.

"Did you bring a guest?"

"My sister-in-law. Tony's younger sister." She looked around. "God knows where she's got to. Hey what happened to Dorothy from Wizard of Oz?"

"The costume was already out so I'm Aphrodite, the Greek goddess of lurve." I stretched the final word to indicate that I was having a good time. Lying often came naturally to me. It was part of the private eye syndrome.

Val took me by surprise when she asked, "What's this I hear of you getting into a bit of a spat with Katya Watkins at CutCost?"

"That's what I love about Haxford. The speed at which the story spreads. It was something and nothing. But how did you hear about it?"

"I did my shopping there this afternoon and most of the staff were talking about it. They were cheering for you, I think. Amongst her workmates, Katya's about as popular as fish 'n' chips at a slimmer's weekend. Honestly, Chrissy, she's a nasty

109

piece of work."

I laughed. "I'd guessed."

"Bit off more than she could chew with you, eh?"

"Just a bit," I lied. "You'll have to excuse me, Val. I'm here for Radio Haxford and I'd better circulate."

I wandered off, thinking about the exchanges with Katya Watkins and as I recalled the incidents, I saw her. She was the redhead talking to Kim.

Before I could get to rescue my friend, Theah intercepted me.

"Heath Mottershaw, Mrs Capper." He offered his hand and I shook it. "But as Theah, I bid you good fortune."

I felt like saying, 'if you're that good, tell me what tomorrow's lottery numbers are.' I didn't of course. That would make me as daft as them.

"Thank you. By the way, just so we know where we're at, I need to interview Heath Mottershaw on Monday, not Theah the flighty or whatever you call yourself."

"Obviously. And by the way, it's Theah the Mighty."

'Flighty' instead of 'mighty' was a deliberate mistake on my part. I was trying to send a subliminal signal that I wasn't really impressed by his silly get up and sillier friends.

He reverted to what I felt was his true accent: proper Haxford. "There'll be scope for the occasional pronouncement from Theah, won't there?"

"I should imagine so, but that'll be up to Eric

Reitman, Mr Mottershaw. I'm just the front man... woman. I don't have any say over editorial policy."

"No, course not." He spotted my empty glass. "Here. Let me get you a top up." Before I could refuse, he snatched the glass from my hand, and disappeared into the throng surrounding the makeshift bar.

I was glad of the opportunity to think of what I would say when he got back. I suppressed a comment to the effect that the words 'part', as in playing one, and 'prat', as in being one, were spelled with the same letters, and by that time, he was back with a fresh glass of cheap shampoo.

Instead, I said, "Tell me, Mr Mottershaw, why the clock?" I gestured at the tower clock stood behind the band and now reading 9:30. How could the time have passed so quickly?

"New Year's Eve," he replied. "The Haxford Larpers have this marquee in place all the time... at least until Barncroft's Farm is sold we do. We're having another soiree on New Year's Eve so we decided to get everything in place all at once." He smiled again. "Would you like an invitation?"

I returned the insincere smile. "Thank you, but no. New Year's Eve is a family time for us. My husband, son, parents, mother-in-law. You understand?" I didn't wait for an answer, but changed the subject. "Has Eric furnished you with a list of the questions I'll put?"

"He has. Straightforward enough and he's giving me the opportunity to push my business efforts. Tell you what, though, I never hear you plugging your Dennis's set up, Haxford Fixers."

"Unseemly," I told him. "Besides, he has enough work coming in as it is without inundating him. If he took on more, I'd never see him."

"And yet, Reggie Monk always announces you as Haxford's only vlogger and blogger and private eye."

The comment seemed totally irrelevant to me. What did my efforts have to do with never seeing Dennis through overwork?

I gave him the same sweet smile, laced with nitric acid, as I'd given his pal, Trippet. "I'm not responsible for Reggie."

"No but that's where my dearly beloved heard of you and it's where she got the idea of hiring you, isn't it?"

As conversation stoppers go, that one was in a class of its own. "She, er, she told you?"

"But of course. You probably never had the pleasure of Adele's company before today, so allow me to tell you about her. She's been a good wife. A Haxford Wife."

I knew what he meant by that. Haxford Wives were the exact antithesis of Stepford Wives. Where the latter were docile, subservient, there to service the requirements of their other halves, Haxford Wives were fiercely independent, deferred to no one, thoroughly, totally in charge of their lives and those of their family, including the theoretical men in command. Thinking about the superficial impression Adele gave me that morning, she slotted right into the role. When she said 'jump' men didn't even bother to ask 'how high'. They just did it to the best of their meagre ability.

Unkind souls would tell you that I'm a Haxford Wife, but it's not strictly true. In order to fulfil the criteria, a Haxford Wife had to married to a Haxford Husband, a man who was under complete control, and I wasn't. True I had ways and means of making Dennis toe the line, but he often argued back and when he had a real strop on him, nothing on earth would make him bow to my, or any woman's, wishes. Why stop at women? He wouldn't bow to anyone's demands, male or female.

It came as a surprise when Mottershaw described his wife as such. He was a salesman. More than that: a *used car* salesman. Such men were usually well-versed in persuasion and maintaining control of any situation. If Adele was the woman he claimed her to be, there was no way he would ever control or persuade her, and when I thought about it, she'd indicated as much when I spoke to her.

"She's concerned over her gran's engagement ring," Mottershaw announced, bringing me out of my reverie. "I can tell you, Mrs Capper, it won't be in any pawnbroker's window. It'll be tucked away at home somewhere. I haven't seen it in who knows how long, and even if I had, there's no way I would have hocked it."

"Even if I take your word for that, Mr Mottershaw, your wife still owes me for the time and effort I've put in."

"That's her concern, not mine." He gave me a weak smile and looked around, and then, in a voice and enunciation perfect for the House of Commons, said, "As the organiser of this evening, I'm duty bound to circulate. If you'll excuse me." He bowed his head and his pointed hat wobbled. For a moment, I thought it was going to fall off, but it stayed in place and he went on his way.

Frankly, I was glad. His switch from Haxford to Queen's English grated slightly on me. With other people, it was a case of, 'here I am, like me or don't'. Dennis, for example, never changed from basic West Yorkshire no matter where we were or who we were with. Reggie Monk was another. As you heard him on the radio, so he was in the pub. Eric Reitman was better educated than most of us, and he never dropped into his native Yorkshire.

Mottershaw on the other hand, was either still playing his schoolboy games or trying to be something he wasn't, which probably amounted to the same thing, and for my money, it made him disingenuous, not to be trusted. Mind, if he really had pinched his wife's grandma's engagement ring, then it went without saying that you couldn't trust him. I go further. He'd just lied about it.

I mentally chastised myself. It was important for any private investigator to maintain an impartial approach to clients and suspects alike. It was unfair to say that Heath Mottershaw had just lied to me without conclusive proof. Then again, I knew of detectives – Paddy Quinn was the best example I could think of – who made a habit of assuming guilt, and in the early stages of any investigation he didn't stop to worry about trivia like evidence. Beyond that, Mottershaw was a used car salesman and exaggeration was a key weapon in their armoury.

So on that basis, I decided (again) that he had

lied to me, and he really did steal his wife's jewellery, and having told me that I wouldn't find it in any hock shop window, I guessed he'd probably sold it and Adele Mottershaw really was paying me for nothing.

Chapter Ten

Having come to this conclusion, I looked around for Jo and she was at the food table with Kim, who had a plate piled high with chicken legs, sausage rolls, dinky pies, beetroot, pickled onions, and so on: bog-standard Haxford fayre for this kind of thrash.

Kim had managed to lose the company of the Virgin Queen and both were now chatting to Medusa whom I recognised right away and I must say, the costume, a plain, dingy green gown, snake-infested wig and a mass of silver (or iron) chains round her neck, suited her.

"Hello, Adele," I said as I joined them. "I thought you didn't care for Heath and his pals?"

"I don't. But I like to keep my eye on him. I noticed you talking to him a few minutes ago. I suppose he denied taking the rings"

"He did. He says you've lost them."

"He would. He's a car salesman, remember. Lying goes with the territory." She bestowed a smile laced with cyanide on Kim. "I'll leave you to it, but remember what I said. He's like all men. A waste of space."

I watched her move on and then asked my friend, "What was that all about?"

"Alden. She doesn't like him. He once fined her

for returning books late."

"I shouldn't worry about it. She doesn't like anyone. So how did you get on with Katya Watkins?"

Even as I asked the question, I noticed a dark frown come to Jo's eyes.

"Oh, Queen Elizabeth the first?" Kim said. "I've known her for yonks. She's about seven or eight years younger than me, but her lot lived on our street when we were growing up. Always was a snooty, bad tempered little cow, even when she was, like, thirteen or fourteen years old. She's one of Motty's mob. Playing silly sods on a weekend. She's a tack, or someone, queen of the witches."

"Aytak," I corrected her, "It's Katya spelled backwards."

"Entirely typical," Jo put in.

Kim nodded and guzzled a mouthful of champagne. "Don't know that it suits her. She was never backward in coming forward. She was showing me her fancy ring. A big stone in a circle of glass. What do they call it?" She thought for a moment. "Gannet."

"You mean garnet."

"Do I? Oh. All right. Anyway, she was telling me it's part and parcel of this wizards and witches thing, she said. It gives her magical powers. Some power. I'll bet she didn't pay more than a tenner for it on Haxford market."

"She? You mean the Haxford Larpers paid..." A memory from my visit to the costume shop leapt into my head and I had to stop and think about my last words. "Although, I don't know. According to

117

Adele Mottershaw, the Larpers pay for their own costumes and stuff, so maybe she did cough up for it herself."

With a half drunken wave, Kim left Jo and me to it.

Finishing her drink, Jo wolfed down a party sausage roll and moved to the table, where she stocked her plate with a couple more, added two chicken drumsticks and some pickle.

I cast an eye to her tummy. "You just peckish or are you eating for two?"

"What? Not likely. No, I didn't get much dinner, and Bernard can't stand pickles, so I'm making sure he won't come near me when we get to bed." She looked around as she chewed on a drumstick. "Boring, this do, Chrissy. No offence, but I wish I'd turned you down."

"I know what you mean. Has Roger Trippet hit on you, yet?"

"No, but I saw him turning the glad eye on you." She giggled. "Even Daniel Craig would be wasting his time with you, wouldn't he?"

I laughed. "I might make an exception in his case, but not dodgy Roger." I sipped more of the cheap shampoo. "So you've had hassle with Katya Watkins, too, have you?"

"How did you guess?"

"I could see it in your eyes when I mentioned her to Kim."

"Never let it be sad that you're not a proper private eye." She smiled. "Katya's just a bitch."

"So what happened between you?"

"I do my weekly shop at CutCost. Well, I used

to. These days, I do it online and that's thanks to her. When I went there, I always used shop and scan."

"Me too. Saves all that queueing at the checkouts."

She nodded her assent. "I always used to treat myself to a small bar of chocolate when I did the job. Do you do that?"

"Now and again. I have to be careful. I'm a self-confessed chocoholic."

"So am I. Anyway, rather than put the chocolate in the bag, where I'd have to dig it out to eat in the car, I used to scan it and put it in my pocket. She spotted me and called for security. Accused me of shoplifting, and when I tried to show her the scanner, she wouldn't listen. Security were ranting about searching my bags and then bringing in the police and in the end I insisted they brought Aidan Compton out. When he got there, I showed him the scanner and he backed down, apologised for the mix up, tore Katya off a strip, but the cow didn't even have the decency to apologise. I warned her if I ever saw her crossing the road, she'd better hurry or I'd mow her down. After that, whenever I went there, she'd be keeping an eye on me, and I had to warn her again and again."

"So you stopped going to the store?"

She nodded. "Mostly. I still call in now and again if there's something urgent we need. Let's face, Haxford's not good for serious supermarkets, is it?"

"Very poor." I sighed. "Time to do the rounds again. It won't be long before I'm ringing Dennis to pick me up."

The evening dragged on, the music became even more boring, Reggie Monk put in a brief appearance as Elvis Presley. I'm not sure how he got in. According to Eric Reitman, he wasn't representing Radio Haxford but I noticed he didn't stick around for long. I spotted Adele exchanging what looked like harsh words with Katya Watkins. Nothing fresh there. Adele Mottershaw didn't seem to do anything but harsh words. Then I bumped into Barry Barnes, son of Benny who ran Benny's Bargain Basement, the cheapest shop in Haxford if you were looking for anything and everything. I paused to exchange a few words with Mr Terence Shakespeare, the mayor of Haxford, and his wife Olga. He was dressed as the duke of Wellington, and she was supposed to be Queen Victoria, but she looked more like Hattie Jacques as Mrs Fezziwig in the Alistair Sim version of A Christmas Carol.

With the time inching past ten o'clock, I was beginning to get as bored as Jo and I was thinking again about ringing Dennis when an ear-splitting scream from the far side of the marquee, the exit where the portaloos were located, pierced the air.

A crowd was already gathering and the security people were struggling to hold the crowds back. Kim caught up with me, and with her clinging onto my toga, I battled my way through, only to come against the bulky arm of one security man.

"Just stay put, missus. There's been an accident."

"Yes? And I'm a police officer. Now get out of the way."

While he puzzled over my lie I brushed his arm to one side and with Kim still hanging onto me, stepped out into the chilly night to find Heath Mottershaw close to the farmhouse, bent over the inert form of Katya Watkins. As I watched, he was reaching out a hand to her. Her knickers were discarded off to one side, giving us a slight clue as to what she might have been doing, but a plainly livid weal around her neck and above the ruff of her Elizabethan costume told me all I needed to know.

I snapped at Mottershaw. "Don't touch her."

"What?" He leapt back as if he'd suffered an electric shock. "And just who do you think—"

"Someone who knows what she's doing." I ducked past the rope cutting off the marquee and toilets from the farmhouse, shouldered him to one side, reached down, pressed a shaking finger to her neck and withdrew my hand. Exactly as I suspected. I glared up at him. "She's dead."

Mottershaw gasped along with some of the other people crowding the area. "Dead? But... She can't be."

"Oh. Right. I've got it wrong have I? Why don't you wave your magic wand and wake her up then?" I glared at him. "She has no pulse. It's a bit of a giveaway, that."

Somehow he managed to pull himself together. "Right. Well, in that case, we'd better get her moved." He faced the security men. "You two—"

"Stay where you are," I barked at the two men concerned before turning on Mottershaw. "You don't move her, you don't touch her. You keep everyone away from her, and you make sure no one leaves."

"But the toilets." He waved a hand at the line of portaloos. "People will need them."

Everything had happened with such speed that I'd forgotten about them. Mottershaw was right. Dead woman or not, people would need to relieve themselves. I signalled to the security men. "You two, get here. Stand in front of her and usher people past to the lavatories. Don't let anyone this side of the ropes."

"Yeah but—"

"What are you? Security officers or is the uniform part of your fancy dress? Just do it." I turned back to Mottershaw. "We need the police out here, now."

"Oh that's ridic—"

"Are you listening to me?" I interrupted for the second time. "I know what I'm talking about, and I know what I'm doing. We need the police out here ASAP, and if you don't call them, I will."

"Yes but…"

I didn't hear the rest of his complaint. I took out my phone and dialled Mandy direct.

"You don't half know how to make my night," she grumbled when I explained the situation. "Any obvious injuries?"

"A weal round her neck. I touched her neck to check for a pulse, but that's all. I've set security people guarding her to make sure we don't get any nosy parkers looking her over."

"Okay, Chrissy. I'll bell Paddy and be with you in about twenty minutes. For now, no one can leave the place."

"Fine. Would you like to tell Heath Mottershaw that? He doesn't believe me."

"Put him on."

I handed my phone to Mottershaw. "Detective Sergeant Hiscoe, Haxford CID," I told him.

He went straight on the attack, but shut up in less than five words as Mandy took over. Obviously, I couldn't hear what she was saying, but I knew her well. She was more than capable of dealing with the Heath Mottershaws of this world. I've said many times that she should be an inspector, but that would involve leaving Haxford, and she loved her home town.

As the call went on, Mottershaw was reduced to occasional responses. "Yes... Yes... I understand..." and I was tempted to laugh but the situation was far too serious.

It called to mind the business at Christmas Manor where I was alone, but the police couldn't get there because the place was snowed in. I was confronted with a crowd of (alleged) business bigwigs, none of whom were happy to accept my authority, even though Paddy Quinn had told them to co-operate, and my only support was Eric Reitman and his wife, Beryl. At least I wouldn't have that problem this time.

Eventually, Mottershaw handed my phone back, muttered, "I have to make an announcement," and from there he began to marshal the security people.

"I've given him instructions, Chrissy," Mandy told me. "No one can leave until we get there, and I'm sorry but that includes you. Paddy will be in seventh heaven when I ring him."

"Not when he learns I'm here, he won't."

She laughed. "I'll tell him and it'll make his night, I reckon. Now, can you tell me any more than you already have?"

"No. I'm sorry."

"Okay. No worries. I'll see you in a bit."

I cut the call, and motioned the security guards to one side, while I looked down on the poor woman. Her face was set in a mask of agony from which I deduced that the assault had been quick, unexpected, and painful. Her eyes were open, staring in sheer disbelief, and I wanted to close them, but that would be against the rules. Her head was crooked to one aside and at an awkward angle, and once again experience told me that she had probably been strangled from behind. Again, it was tempting to roll her over and take a look, but Paddy would flay me alive for such an action.

"Her knuckleduster's missing."

It was Kim, keeping her voice down and pointing at Katya's left hand.

"What?"

"The cheap and nasty ring I was telling you about."

I activated the torch on my smartphone and then bent to check. Kim was right. I could see the marks where the ring had been almost torn from her finger, a grazing of the knuckle.

Suspicion entered my head. Hadn't I seen Katya arguing with Adele half an hour earlier? "Describe this ring to me again."

"I told you. A big garnie with bits of glass all

124

round it."

I felt a flush of relief. A garnet. Had it been a sapphire…

"Do us a favour, Kim. If I have to stand out here all night, I'm gonna freeze. Can you get my coat for me?" I handed her my raffle ticket.

"No problem."

She disappeared through the crowd and as I returned to studying Katya's body, the mayor's voice cut into my thoughts.

"This is damned inconvenient."

He was stood behind me, arguing with Mottershaw.

"I'm sorry, Mr Mayor, but the police have insisted."

"Yes, well, it's still a flaming nuisance. We were on our way home."

I'd never been a fan of politicians, local or national, and whatever trust I once had in them disappeared altogether after the McCrudden affair. His worship's selfishness grated on me and I found it impossible to keep my mouth shut. "So inconsiderate of her, wasn't it? You'd think she'd have more regard for others before getting herself murdered, wouldn't you?"

"Now listen—"

"No, you listen. This isn't the council chamber. Out here, you're no different to the rest of us. This woman has been murdered and I believe she's been robbed and the police will treat each and every one of us as a suspect until they're satisfied otherwise."

Shakespeare's chubby features darkened. "Who do you think you are, talking to me like that?"

"One of the idiots who cast her cross and helped you land your job."

"I'll be talking to Langdon about you."

I wasn't impressed by threats of him haranguing the head of Radio Haxford either. "Would you like to borrow my phone to ring him?"

The argument could have gone on, but for Mottershaw, who asked, "How do you know she's been murdered and robbed?"

"I told you, I'm an ex-police officer, and I know how to recognise the signs. Now please be patient, all of you. Mandy Hiscoe won't be long."

In fact, it was a couple of uniforms and my son Detective Constable Simon Capper who turned up first, and he did not look too pleased about it.

"When we have a suspicious death, I expect Mandy to drag me out, I don't expect to find it's my own mother calling it in."

"Right, Simon. The next time I come across a body, I'll tell Mandy not to tell you who I am. How are Naomi and Bethany?"

"They're fine, Mam. Now can we concentrate on the body?"

The uniforms pressed the onlookers back and as I moved away, Simon got straight to work, pulling on a pair of forensic gloves and checking for a pulse, then rolling her body over her to look for signs of more wounding.

Watching him at work, I felt an immense glow of pride. When he left school, Dennis expected him to take an apprenticeship with Haxford Fixers, but Simon had his heart firmly set on the police, and three years later, after working his way through university, he signed on. He could have opted for fast track graduate status, but he refused. A Haxforder through and through, he wanted to work in his own town, so he chose the slow route. He was promoted over New Year two years previously, and was now a fully-fledged DC working with Mandy. He followed his mother's footsteps and went further. I never wanted CID.

Mandy arrived five minutes later and barely had time for the customary greetings, before pushing her way to the front and going into a whispered conversation with Simon for him to bring her up to speed. Uniforms pushed the crowd, of which I was one, further back, and the medical examiner was a minute behind Mandy. From where I stood, well back from the scene but at the front of the crowd, I watched him carry out his preliminary examination and then roll Katya over again.

I came away and joined the general throng. It was so crowded in that marquee that I couldn't see Jo anywhere and Kim had moved to stand with Alden.

I was one of the earliest to be interviewed, despite Terence Shakespeare's protest that he was more important. I distinctly heard Simon tell him to shut up and wait his turn, and Shakespeare's warning that he would report my son to the station commander. I don't know what Simon said to that, but it was likely something along the lines of 'please yourself'.

"You're the most observant," Mandy told me, "so I need as much information as you can give me."

It didn't amount to much over what I'd told her on the phone, but I did tell her of the assumed argument I'd seen between Katya and Adele.

When we were through, Mandy let me go and I collected my coat from Kim, then stepped out of the front and rang Dennis.

"It's only eleven o'clock. You said after midnight and I were just gonna get a bit of kip."

"Yes, well, things have gone haywire, Dennis. A woman's been killed."

"You never told me they were doing Christmas sacrifices these days." He laughed at his supposed joke.

"It's not funny, Dennis. Just get in the car and come for me. I'll be waiting by the marquee."

He turned up twenty minutes later in my Renault. "I figured it's a bit warmer than the Morris," he explained when I climbed in.

He was right. I was glad of the heater as he turned round and made for home.

"So who's this who's been iced, then?" he asked, and when I told him, his eyes popped. "Jeebers. Isn't that her you had a coupla barneys with in CutCost?"

I agreed that it was and fell silent for the rest of the journey home. When I got there, I didn't waste much time. I drank a welcome, much needed cup of tea, swallowed two paracetamol, and as I got ready for bed, I noted one of my earrings was missing. I didn't have the energy to deal with it then, so I put a couple of studs in, and I was in bed for just turned midnight. Dennis had to be up for work no later than seven so he wasn't far behind me, but by then I was asleep.

The next thing I knew it was three in the morning and the doorbell was ringing and ringing and ringing. Dennis answered it and even though I was still half asleep I would swear I heard Mandy's voice arguing with my old man.

Still groggy, I rolled out of bed and made my unsteady way to the front door where Dennis was, indeed, arguing with Mandy and Fliss Keele. Odd that. They usually only came in gender matched pairs when they were delivering bad news or about to make an arrest. But they surely couldn't...

Mandy laid eyes on me. "Christine Capper, you're wanted down at the station for questioning on the murder of Katya Watkins."

Chapter Eleven

That woke me up.

"What? Are you out of your mind, Mandy?"

She remained steadfast, and with great formality, said, "You have to come with us, Mrs Capper. If you refuse, I'll have no option but to arrest you."

"For the umpteenth time, it's three o'clock in the perishing morning," Dennis complained.

"I'm aware of the time, Mr Capper." Mandy switched her focus to me. "I'll give you a few minutes to dress and then we can go."

"Mandy—"

She dropped the formality. "Chrissy, the sooner we get this over with, the better off we'll all be. Now let's move it."

I'd been there often enough during my eight years with the police and I knew she was right. "I'll just get dressed."

Less than half an hour later, my few possessions taken from me, I was in one of the interview rooms opposite Mandy and Paddy. They were in a grim mood, but theirs was nothing compared to mine. I was still sleepy, but sufficiently awake and aware to meet them head on if I had to.

They identified themselves for the benefit of the

recorder, I identified myself and Paddy went on to outline the situation.

"As you're aware, the body of Katya Watkins was discovered close to the farmhouse in the vicinity of the temporary toilets at Barncroft's Farm a little after ten o'clock last night—"

"I was the one who called it in," I interrupted.

"You were. Medical examination concluded that she had been strangled using a narrow, rope chain made of polished, stainless steel. We took statements from everyone at the Festival Ball, including you. Indeed, yours was one of the first statements taken by Sergeant Hiscoe, and after you gave it, you were allowed to leave. Sometime after, a witness told us that they had seen you with Ms Watkins by the farmhouse wall and although the witness couldn't hear, it looked as if you we arguing—"

"It wasn't me—"

Paddy held up his hand to interrupt me. "Kindly allow me to finish, Mrs Capper. You'll have your say in due course." He consulted his notes. "In the opinion of the medical examiner, Ms Watkins was killed where she lay. Other witnesses indicated that you were carrying a clutch purse with a rope chain made – presumably – of stainless steel, and we're going to need to see that to ascertain whether it matches the pattern of the scars on Ms Watkins's neck. Another witness told us that you had a blazing argument with Ms Watkins at CutCost earlier in the day and a similar confrontation yesterday… forgive me, Thursday. Finally, Mrs Adele Mottershaw, a one to one private tutor, whom we contacted on the advice of her husband, Heath Mottershaw, told us that she engaged you as a private investigator a couple of days ago to look for a valuable sapphire and diamond engagement ring, which she said was stolen from her and that one of the people possibly involved in that theft, was Ms Watkins. A cursory examination of Ms Watkins revealed that something had been roughly removed from her finger. This was confirmed by Ms Kimberly Aspinall, a friend of yours, who had spoken with Ms Watkins earlier in the evening and noticed that Ms Watkins was wearing an ostentatious, expensive looking ring, but when she saw the woman's body, that ring was missing. Searches of the deceased's clothing and the immediate area around the toilets and farmhouse have not turned up the ring." Paddy pushed his notes to one side, rested his elbows on the table and with his hands clasped, leaned slightly forward. "The way we see it, Christine, you lost it altogether when you found her wearing the ring. We know she could be a forceful, argumentative woman, but you decided to show her who was the more forceful. Just tell us, luv. Get it off your chest. It'll go so much easier for you when it comes to court." And with that, he sat back.

I risked a glance at Mandy. She was obviously uncomfortable with the situation, and I knew that she was acting on Paddy's orders. If it had been up to her, she would have spoken to me at home rather than dragging me to the station in the early hours of the morning. But that was Paddy all over. He had always been hasty, sometimes to the point of ignoring a suspect's rights altogether. I knew him well and if Paddy had to be up and at it at this early hour, there was no way any suspect would be permitted to laze around in bed.

He wasn't the only one who could play silly games, and if my years in the police and as a private eye had taught me anything, it was how to divide and conquer.

"Are you through," I asked and he nodded. I switched focus to Mandy. "You've not had much to say for yourself. Do you believe even half of this claptrap?"

She didn't answer, but her ears coloured slightly and that told me how accurate my analysis was.

I went on the attack. "First things first. Send a car to my place, knock Dennis up – if he's gone back to bed – and bring the handbag down. There were plenty of people taking photographs at that do, and I'm sure you've got your share of them. You'll be able to identify the bag in question, but if there are any doubts, tell Dennis it's hung over one of the kitchen chairs. The time I got home last night, I couldn't be bothered tidying it away in the wardrobe. I bought that bag brand new yesterday – pardon me, Thursday – from Hattie's Handbags on the market and she'll verify that and identify the bag when she opens up this morning." I glared at Mandy. "If you'd said something, I'd have brought it with me."

Again Mandy did not answer, but she picked up the phone and while I rounded on Paddy, she muttered into the receiver.

I glowered at the inspector. "Almost every

133

word you said came right out of your backside."

"We have a witness."

"Who saw what? A woman in a toga arguing with another woman? There were any number of women there wearing togas, and I don't know who your witness saw, but it was not me—"

"The witness named you," Mandy interrupted. She was obviously still smarting from my darts a few minutes ago.

"And you're not going to tell me who he or she is, are you?" Their silence was answer enough. "Your eyewitness is lying... or mistaken. I repeat, it was not me. Yes, I had sharp exchanges with Katya Watkins in CutCost yesterday and the day before. I don't know who told you about it, but it was not the blazing row you suggested. But it was enough to ensure that I purposely avoided Katya last night. Moving on, yes Adele Mottershaw hired me to track down her grandmother's engagement ring, but that ring was a sapphire and diamond cluster. According to my friend, Kim Aspinall, Katya was wearing a cheap dress ring of garnet and glass. Am I so stupid, or was I so drunk on a couple of glasses of cheap champagne, that I couldn't tell the difference between garnet, which is red, and sapphire, which is blue? You have nothing, Mr Quinn, other than the word of a supposed witness, and considering the amount of free booze flowing in that tent, his or her account is wide open to question."

"Well, we should know one way or the other quite soon," Mandy said. "I've sent a car to pick up this bag. It should be back in, say, twenty minutes."

"And what will you do then, Paddy?" I

demanded. "When you're proven wrong? Go down on your knees and beg my forgiveness for dragging me out of bed in the middle of the night? For god's sake, you've known me long enough to realise this is not me."

"We're following a legitimate line of enquiry," he snapped, "and it doesn't matter how long I've known you, I can't let personal considerations hamper our investigation." He leaned forward again. "If we, that is Sergeant Hiscoe and I, feel that there's a case to answer, I'll call for a chief inspector from Huddersfield to take over the inquiry because of my prior knowledge of you."

"And if there isn't a case to answer, I'm not likely to get an apology, am I?"

"Let's all just calm down," Mandy insisted.

"Sergeant—"

She cut Paddy off. "I'm sorry, sir, but this is getting too personal, and you've already said, we can't allow such opinions or feelings to get in the way." She stopped the recording and then rounded on me. "And you're just as bad, Chrissy. So we got you out of bed in the middle of the night. It's a murder inquiry. We're doing our job, and you've been involved in law and order and investigative work long enough to know that we can't sit on it until morning. Not when we have a witness statement which points at you." She paused to let her words sink in. "Why don't we all calm down? I'll order some tea and if Mr Quinn is agreeable, let's see what you might be able to tell us about the Festival Ball."

Her words made sense, and a grumbling silence

fell over the room while we waited for delivery of the canteen tea almost ten minutes later.

Once we were settled, Paddy ordered the recorder to be started again, and then posed the question Mandy had suggested.

"There isn't much I can tell you. I was there as a representative of Radio Haxford and Joanne Petheridge was my guest. To be frank, I found it all rather boring. I spoke to Heath Mottershaw twice, Roger Trippet once, I had a chat with Val Wharrier and her mother, and I had brief exchanges with Terence Shakespeare, the mayor, and one or two other people. That's about it."

"You were also quite abrupt with the mayor," Paddy pointed out. "He told us so."

"Because he was whining over Sergeant Hiscoe's insistence that everyone stay there until the police arrived. I also crossed swords with Heath Mottershaw and the security people on the same issue."

"One of those security men told us you said you were a police officer."

"He misheard me," I lied. "I said I was an ex-police officer. Listen, Mr Quinn, at that point, security hadn't a clue what they were doing. Heath Mottershaw was about to move Katya's body so people wouldn't gawp when they used the toilets. The idiot didn't even realise she was dead. Someone had to take control until your people arrived. And just to harp on the matter I don't recall you objecting when I took charge at Christmas Manor when you couldn't get there for the snow. In fact, it was you who put me in charge."

136

"Different circumstances," Mandy said. "But, all right, we can see your point. Let's move on. You say you didn't speak to Katya all evening?"

"We had the arguments at CutCost, didn't we? Whoever told you about those was telling the truth. I didn't want to get into another argument with her. Remember, I was representing Radio Haxford. If I got into a proper ruck with anyone, it would lead to an uncomfortable interview with James Langdon on Monday morning. So, yes, as I told you, I purposely avoided Katya all evening. I think Jo Petheridge, Val Wharrier, and Kim Aspinall will confirm that."

"We'll speak to them," Paddy insisted.

At that moment, the phone rang. Mandy lifted the receiver, listened, and when the call was ended, she stood up. "The bag's here, sir. I'll go check it out."

She left and with the recorder again switched off, Paddy said, "Tell me about this business between you and Adele Mottershaw... and remember, you're looking at a potential murder charge, so I don't want to hear about client confidentiality."

Over the next few minutes I told him exactly what had transpired between Adele and me at her home, and detailed my slender efforts to find the missing ring.

Paddy was doubtful. "She says her husband stole it?"

"I know how you feel. I couldn't understand it either, but she said his business is in trouble and he was looking to shore up his cash flow."

"And you've confirmed that?"

I shook my head. "Not in so many words. I spoke to Dennis and his partners. They do quite a bit of business with Mottershaw, servicing and valeting the cars he's sold, and they said they haven't had anything from him in weeks. It's the cost of living thing, isn't it? People don't have the money to spare for cars. I should know. Dennis and I are not exactly hard up, but I'm running round in a ten-year-old Renault."

Paddy was silent for a while and then spoke up. "If I assume you're innocent – and I'm not saying you are – is there any way you can think of in which this stolen ring might be linked to the Katya Watkins's murder?"

"Not without more information. There are any number of scenarios, possibilities. I mean you might suspect that Mottershaw was involved with Katya, but Adele is a tough nut and she never gave any indication that she suspected anything between them. Look. Paddy, if you think it might help, I have a photograph of the ring on my phone." I aimed a finger at the evidence bag containing my phone, purse and door keys. The only items Mandy had allowed me to bring with me.

Paddy opened the bag, took out my smartphone and handed it to me. I rooted through the menus, found the photograph Adele had bluetoothed to me, and passed it back to him.

He spent a little time studying it, and then asked, "This is worth, how much? A couple of thou'?"

I shrugged. "So Adele claims, yes. It doesn't matter to me, Paddy. For all I care, it could be worth fifty pence. She'll pay me for the time I put in trying to trace it."

It was as if I hadn't said anything. "And this wasn't the ring Katya was allegedly wearing last night?"

I could see Paddy set the question as a trap. If I said 'no' he could challenge me that I had spoken to her during the evening and I'd already said I hadn't. "For the second time, I don't know. I purposely avoided her last night. Kim told me the ring was garnet surrounded by glass. She reckoned Katya won't have paid more than ten pounds for it on the market, and if that's right, then it won't have been garnet. It would have been red glass."

He frowned. "Then why would anyone bother nicking it or even killing her for it?"

"Because they might have thought it was valuable." I sighed. "To get this debate back to where we started, I wouldn't have killed her for it. Even if it had been the real thing, blue instead of red, I would have made a note of it and reported back to Adele Mottershaw. That's what I get paid to do."

"Let's not get into that. Not while Mandy's out of the room."

I should have guessed his reaction. "Well, I don't know what more I can say. As far as I'm concerned, until you have information or uncover evidence to the contrary, the theft of this ring has no bearing on Katya's death."

More silence. I risked a quick glance at the clock on the wall, which now read 4:15. At best I'd had three hours' sleep. Dennis would be up for work in a couple of hours and he would not have had much more rest than me. Anyone with any sense would take the day off especially as it was a Saturday, but then, common sense and the men of Haxford – especially in the shape of Dennis Capper – didn't always come as a full set.

The door opened, Mandy popped her head in and indicated to Paddy that he should join her. He excused himself, left the interview room and closed the door behind him. I knew what was happening. The comparison between my bag and the wound on Katya's neck was inconclusive and they were planning their tactics. If it was similar, I could expect more pressure when they returned. If it was not, then they would veer off in other directions to press for a confession.

Either way, I was not worried. I knew I was innocent and somewhere along the line, they would realise it too.

The door opened, they returned and started the recorder again.

Paddy took the lead. "The current situation is that the marks on Katya's neck do not appear to match the chain on your bag." He hurried on before I could gloat. "This is not definitive. Your bag and Katya's body need closer, forensic examination before we can be absolutely certain, so you're not off the hook yet."

"You know damn well it isn't me."

He pressed on as if I hadn't spoken. "Tomorrow – pardon me – today we'll send a team out to your house to search for other bags which may have a chain that does match. If you object, I'll ask for a warrant to search your house."

"I don't mind. Better yet, why not send them out now and they can give me a lift home. Even better, rather than wasting your time and police money searching for evidence to charge me, why don't you talk to your witness again, and find out why he or she named me. Best of all, give me his or her name and I'll talk to him... her... it."

"I can't do that, and you know I can't. You're free to leave, Christine, but remember, you are still under caution."

As I stood he delivered another warning.

"You must not, under any circumstances, discuss this with your son. He's family, I can't stop you seeing him, but he's also a serving police officer, and if you try to talk to him about the case, you may very well jeopardise his career. Am I making myself clear?"

"Abundantly."

Chapter Twelve

If I felt rough when I got home about a quarter to five that morning, it was nothing compared to the way I felt when Dennis brought home the Saturday evening edition of the Haxford Recorder and I read that front page.

When I got back from the police station, I settled in the kitchen with a cup of tea, trying to calm down, trying to put together what might have happened the previous night, ferreting through recollections of the familiar faces for the one who might have deliberately identified me to the police.

Deliberately? Definitely. True, there were many people at the ball I didn't know, but would they have identified me by name? It was possible, granted, but it was much more likely to be someone who did know me, had me in their sights and saw the opportunity to drop me in it. There was also the possibility that it was the real killer who by coincidence was dressed like me, and decided to create herself an alibi by accusing me.

Herself? If such was the case, then it had to be a woman. As far as I could judge, the only people wearing togas were female.

Dennis crawled out of bed at six (as always) and I spent a little time with him, telling him of my adventures (poor choice of word) at the police station. He looked worn out. He'd had no more than four hours' sleep and that was disturbed when the police came for my handbag.

I suggested he take the day off, but he refused. "Too much work on," he said.

I went to bed soon after, but sleep came only slowly as I turned the events of the night over and over and over in my mind. I guess it must have been almost seven when I finally fell asleep only to be woken at midday by the police search team.

Mandy was leading them, but her aside, I knew the other officers, all uniforms, by sight, if not by name. They spent an hour or more going through the house, and their only query had nothing to do with the handbag, but concerned a ruby ring which they found in my jewellery boxes.

"It's mine," I told Mandy, "and Dennis or Simon or Naomi will be able to confirm that. Dennis bought it for my fortieth birthday and I've talked to both Simon and Naomi about it often enough for them to know. What's more, if you look at it, the stone is in a gold clasp, and it's not surrounded by glass or diamonds or whatever Katya's ring was supposed to look like."

She accepted my explanation without comment.

It was an odd situation. Mandy and I had been friends for many years, but while her team were searching the house, she was all business and did not speak to me at all, except to clear up the query concerning the ring. When they left the house and set about searching both my car and the garage, she went with them, leaving a uniform with me (to ensure I didn't try to hide potentially incriminating evidence).

When they were finally through, they asked for the toga, I handed it over, and she bagged it up, handed it to the search team leader, and said to me, "We'll have it checked for forensic traces, and assuming there's nothing we'll get it back to you."

With that, the time approaching quarter to three, she dismissed the team and sent them on their way. Only then did she join me at the kitchen table.

"I'm sorry, Chrissy."

"And I'm not?" I laced my response with acid.

"If it hadn't been for this witness, we wouldn't be in this position."

"And you still won't tell me who it is."

"Not won't. Can't. And let's not pretend you don't know that." She stood up. "Let me put the kettle on."

"Stay where you are." Now I stood up. "I'll do it. That way you'll know where to look for my fingerprints."

I made tea for us and rejoined her at the table. I had no idea what to say to her. On the one hand, she was one of my best friends, but on the other, she was trying to convict me of murder.

I needn't have worried. She had plenty to say. "I took the witness statement, and I knew right away that it was wrong. I even told Paddy that, and as you know, most of the time, I'm ready to argue the toss with him, but as he pointed out, this person actually named you. From there we had no choice but to bring you in. If, as I expect, we clear you, we then have to query how or why the witness could have made such a mistake."

"Deliberately springs to mind," I retorted. "But I can't make a judgement on that because I don't know who it is."

"And you won't get to know. Not from me, anyway, and if you get the name from anyone else you'll need to let me know who told you."

"Typical. Not only can they slag me off, but I'm—"

"It's the way it works, Chrissy. For god's sake, get the knot out of your knickers. I'm putting my job on the line here, just talking to you. We've been besties since I can't remember when, and I'm trying to save your hide. I don't believe you're guilty, and neither does Paddy, but because we know you so well, because we've actually used you to help us out in the past, we have to do it by the book. We can't allow the smallest hint of favouritism."

She was right. I knew she was right. In her position, I would do exactly the same. It was time to back off, so I acquiesced. "All right, you win." I found some fire. "But don't expect me to sit back and mind my own business. I will look into this."

That seemed to satisfy her. "We guessed you would and we can't stop you. We wouldn't want to. But do remember, anything you learn, you have to bring it to us."

"Guaranteed."

Mandy left and I sank into a depression, asking myself over and over again how this could happen. When it came to routine matters such as cleaning and tidying, feeding Cappy the Cat, I carried out the duties as an automaton, without enthusiasm, almost

145

without thought, running on automatic pilot. Somewhere along the line, I remembered my missing earring and set about searching the kitchen, conservatory and bedroom for it.

That was just after three o'clock and while I was rooting round the bedroom, I noticed people beginning to gather at the end of our drive. I didn't recognise any of them, but the abundance of professional cameras told me they were press and I couldn't understand why they were there unless...

No. Not even Paddy in his worst moods would name me, and I knew Mandy wouldn't.

Dennis arrived about half past four and hampered by the darkness and the crowd, he struggled to get his car into the drive. When he finally made it and climbed out, he went back to the gate, and gave them a serious piece of his mind. Dennis did not use bad language, but I heard some of his ranting and he made an exception in this case.

After taking his boots off in the garage, he came in through the side door, his face like thunder. I made him a mug of tea, and when I returned to the table, he tossed the early evening edition of the Haxford Recorder on the table.

That's when I read that shocking story on the front page.

ARREST IN WATKINS MURDER

Local personality, Christine Capper, known throughout Haxford for her weekly vlog and her interviews on Radio Haxford, was arrested in the early hours of this morning suspected of killing Katya Watkins during the Haxford Christmas Festival Ball at Barncroft's Farm last night.

Ms Watkins, a checkout supervisor at CutCost, was found strangled close to the temporary toilets at about 10:15 last night, and initial inquiries led Detective Inspector Patrick Quinn of West Yorkshire CID to take Mrs Capper in for questioning on suspicion of committing the crime.

"We have been speaking to a woman concerning last night's event. She is currently helping with our inquiries, and I'm sorry, but I can't say any more than that at this moment."

The suspect was later identified as Christine Capper.

We'll bring you updates on this story as it develops.

In a paroxysm of fury I scrunched the paper up and threw it across the kitchen.

"Steady, lass, I haven't read it yet."

"Well, I've read enough." I snatched up my phone and punched Mandy's icon on the home screen.

"Chrissy, I told you—"

"When were you going to tell me you'd named me to the press?"

"No one's named—"

"They're camped on my flaming doorstep. My name's all over the front page of the Recorder. Who else knew but you and Paddy?"

"Hang on, Chrissy, hang on. Paddy wouldn't do that and I certainly haven't."

"Someone has, and it has to be someone from Haxford police station."

"I'll look into it."

"Yes, well, you'd better get some people out

147

here to deal with the press gang. They're blocking the street off."

I didn't wait for her to reply again. I cut the call and threw the phone on the table.

Dennis, meantime, had smoothed out the paper and was about to start reading the classifieds but I snatched it from him.

"Hey. If I did that to you—"

"You can have it back in a minute."

I turned to the front page again, looking for the one thing which, in a fit of temper, I'd not bothered to check. The reporter's byline.

And there it was. Lizzie Finister. *The suspect was later identified as Christine Capper.* Lizzie, rotten cow, Finister. The woman I'd unseated as the resident agony aunt on Radio Haxford. Yes, and even though I had been offered the job rather than having applied for it, she'd never really forgiven me, had she?

And was she out there right now? I would lay money on it.

I stormed through to the front room, and looked through the window at the crowd. As soon as I appeared, the cameras started flashing away and in the stroboscopic lights I could see Lizzie, stood right at the front, firing away with her compact camera.

Ignoring the cold weather, forgetting about my fatigue, fired by anger, I marched out of the house and up to the gates. I was bombarded by a cacophony of questions. I ignored them all. My sights were fixed firmly on that smug half smile plastered across Lizzie Finister's face.

Lowering the camera, pushing forward her pocket recorder, she opened her mouth to add to the welter of unintelligible questions coming at me.

She never got the chance to say anything before my fist landed in her trap. Her lip burst, she staggered back, but couldn't go anywhere because of the crowd behind her. That forced her to bounce forward again, and I drew my fist back to aim another blow at her. Then Dennis grabbed my arm and dragged me back.

"Get your flaming hands off me," I screamed.

"Knock it off, Chrissy. You're in enough trouble as it is."

He was big man, my husband. Way bigger and stronger than me, and with camera flashes lighting up the drive, he pulled me back towards the house. Once inside he let me go, slammed and locked the door, and the flat of my hand took him across the cheek.

"Don't you ever lay your hands on me—"

"SHUT UP!" Dennis's roar could probably be heard in Haxford.

"That's it. I've had enough of your—"

He cut me off a second time. "I haven't even started."

Dennis and I had been together thirty years, give or take, and I couldn't recall ever seeing him so angry. Not with me, anyway.

He launched into his attack. "Do you know how much trouble you've just landed yourself in?"

"She named me."

"And? Who gives a flying one? You know you haven't done nowt, and she's the one who'll have to

149

back down. At least she was before you smacked her in the gob. That's assault and she'll bring the filth in for sure. And she has enough witnesses to nail your stupid backside to the cell walls." He stormed off towards the kitchen, paused at the door, and turned back to glare at me. "You're supposed to be the intelligent one in this house."

The shaft struck home like an arrow and brought with it the awful common sense of every word he had said. Lizzie Finister goaded me in print and I'd made the worst possible mistake. I reacted. Reacting was the correct way of dealing with it, but a smack in the mouth was the wrong kind of reaction. As Dennis suggested, I should have ignored it, waited until Paddy and Mandy cleared my name, and then torn her apart on my vlog.

Hindsight. Not much use when you think about it.

I followed Dennis into the kitchen, where he had put two beakers on the table. "I've made you some tea."

"Dennis—"

"Sit down, drink your tea, and calm down, and let's think about what we're gonna tell plod when they turn up."

I did as he instructed, took a mouthful of tea, and shrugged. "What can I tell them? It'll have to be the truth, and like you said, she has plenty of witnesses."

"Aye, but there's truth and there's the whole truth. Don't tell 'em more than they need to know. Anyroad up, Mandy should be able to pull a few strings for you shouldn't she?"

"Yes. Especially the one that's tightening round my neck."

About ten minutes later, Sonny Scott and Fliss Keele turned up. Before knocking on our door, they got rid of the press crowd, but then got Lizzie Finister into their car to take her statement. Once that was done, we watched Lizzie drive away, and the two uniforms came to the side door, where Dennis let them into the kitchen.

"She was provoked, Sonny," I heard Dennis say as he led them in.

"We need a statement, Dennis. Sorry, mate, but that's the script."

It didn't take long. I admitted punching her, and I gave them my reasons, but even before we were finished, I knew Sonny would have to report it.

"Right, Mrs Capper," he said with great formality. "You will be reported for assault—"

"And what about her? Finister?" Dennis interrupted. "She named and shamed our lass. Does she get done an'all?"

"That's a civil matter, Dennis," I told him. "Punching her is criminal."

"Correct," Sonny agreed. "And as you know, our hands are tied. You will be reported for assault and it'll be up to the station commander whether it goes any further." He put away his bits and pieces and he and Fliss prepared to leave. "If you want my personal opinion, Chrissy, I'd say you did right. Someone should shut that loudmouth up." He gave me a slightly encouraging smile. "But if anyone asks, I'll deny having said that."

Chapter Thirteen

As I expected, the Haxford Recorder went to town on both the murder of Katya Watkins and my attack on Lizzie Finister. By the time the Monday morning issue was up and running on the paper's website, my name was lumped with every great villain from history including Hitler, Pol Pot and based on their handling of the covid crisis, the entire cabinet from when Boris Johnson was Prime Minister.

I rang Ian Noiland, the managing editor but he wouldn't talk to me, so I emailed him direct, warning him that when my name was cleared, I would hang him and his cheap rag out to dry.

I had other concerns. I was due to interview Heath Mottershaw at ten, and I needed to be dressed and ready.

Were those famous last words? Not much.

Eric Reitman rang at nine and told me in no uncertain terms that Mottershaw had refused to sit through an interview with me.

"It doesn't end there, Chrissy," he said. "I had a call from Langdon over the weekend. He wants to see you at ten this morning. There's no debate, no argument. If you're not here, he'll just shut you down, tear up your contract, but he's duty bound to hear you out before he takes any action. I don't want to lose you, but please, Chrissy, please be here."

So I agreed.

I'd had run ins with Langdon, the station controller, in the past, and I had the feeling that I would come out of it with the messy end of the stick, but I was so steamed up that I really didn't care. What was the worst he could do? Fire me? Fine. As long as he paid me, I didn't really give a hoot, and notwithstanding Eric's support, Radio Haxford would struggle to find an agony aunt as popular as me.

I would have to be 'dolled up' for the cancelled, Mottershaw interview, but for what I fancied would be an acrimonious meeting with Langdon, I dragged on a pair of denims and a woolly jumper. If he didn't like it, he could do the other.

I had it half right. He was dressed in his usual business suit, but he didn't care how I looked when I walked into his top floor office just before ten. The tone of the meeting was the bit I got right.

"Sit down, Capper," he ordered.

"Thank you, Langdon."

The curt use of his surname was deliberate and it had the desired effect. His features, already grim, darkened further and he responded as I expected him to. "It's Mr Langdon to you."

We'd had exactly the same argument the last time he tried to railroad me and I maintained a similar stance. "And it's Mrs Capper, to you. According to Eric Reitman, you want to hear my side of the lies the Haxford Recorder spewed."

"Lies? From all I've heard, there's no lie about you having been arrested for murder, and there's no

153

mistaking Lizzie Finister's injuries after you punched her."

"There you go, you see," I replied. "You should try better reading material than Noiland's rag. They are lying. I was NOT arrested for murder. I was questioned after someone claimed to see me commit murder. It's not true and the police don't believe it, but obviously they're duty bound to interview me, which they did. As for Finister, she identified me in the Recorder, and she had no right to do that, so I punched her in the mouth to persuade her to keep it shut in future. Or perhaps I should have kicked her between the legs in an effort to persuade her to keep those shut instead."

That final crude comment was so unlike me that I found it hard to believe I'd said it. I wasn't even sure it had any basis in reality. I didn't know Lizzie that well.

Langdon was not impressed. "Ms Finister was reporting the news."

"She was lying. She was also speaking out of turn. And she works for Radio Haxford, doesn't she? She took over Lost Friends from me." I decided that I'd already invented Lizzie as a tart, so I might as well add a little painful cream. "Here you are harassing me for things I haven't done, yet you're happy to use a reporter who's free with her favours as long as it gets her the story?"

He waved a dismissive hand at my objection. "Finister doesn't work in news. And your guilt or innocence doesn't matter. Your actions, particularly your assault on Finister and your harassment of Heath Mottershaw on Friday evening, have brought this station into disrepute, and as such, I'm terminating you contract forthwith."

"Hang on, hang on. What harassment of Heath Mottershaw. I had a brief conversation with him."

"During which you belittled his LARP activities and—"

"I did nothing of the kind. I simply said I wanted to interview him, not his stupid role-playing alter-ego."

"You also questioned him on a missing ring his wife had engaged you to find."

"I did nothing of the kind." In truth, I couldn't remember whether I had mentioned it or not. "I stopped him moving the dead woman's body, I insisted he call the police and when he dithered, I called them instead. That's it."

"Not according to him. In any event you were there as a representative of Radio Haxford, and you had no business shoving your nose into anything else. You're finished, Capper. Now clear off."

I stood up and leaned over his desk. "No, Langdon. You're finished. When I clear my name, which I will, I'll expose you and your dictatorial attitude to all and sundry." I turned and marched to the door, where I paused and faced him again. "I'll expect to be paid to the end of my contract."

"Expect again. You'll be paid what we owe you."

Determined to have the last word, I said, "We'll see about that," and then I turned, marched out and slammed the door behind me.

Ignoring the astonishment on his PA's face, I hurried down the stairs and made for the exit.

I'd been with the station for over a year and a half and I enjoyed my time with the crew, not to mention the modicum of fame my spots had brought me. I'd made some good friends, Eric and Reggie to name but two, and I had secured other work, private eye work off my air time. Now it was over. And I knew that Langdon wouldn't be slow to let the media know the what and why. I felt like crying.

Eric stopped me as I made for the exit. "Christine, whatever is the matter?"

I was near to tears, but I managed to hold them back. "That... that arse, has fired me." It was strong language coming from me, but I was past caring. "I'm innocent, Eric. I did nothing and he and the flaming Haxford Recorder are pillorying me for it. Well, they haven't heard the last of it. Now, if you'll excuse me, I'm officially persona non grata at Radio Haxford."

"Wait. Christine, please wait. Let me have a word with him."

"The only words you should have for him are unrepeatable in polite company. I'll bid you goodbye, Eric."

As always, when feeling sorry for myself, I felt pangs of hunger, so my first port of call was Terry's Tea Bar, where at least, he had a sympathetic welcome for me.

"Have the filth got their heads screwed on the right way, or what?" he asked as he passed me a cup of tea and put a teacake in the toaster for me.

"I'm not allowed to talk about it, Terry."

"The Recorder are doing all the talking, aren't they? And is it right you lamped Lizzie Finister?"

I nodded. "I'm afraid so."

"Good on you. It's time someone put one on her."

I collected my toasted teacake and took this acid view to a table where I sat wrapped in self-pity. Why Terry had a downer on her, why he inadvertently supported Sonny Scott's opinion, I don't know. Perhaps she'd castigated his catering skills at some point. Or perhaps it was because he didn't like the idea of her slagging off his favourite customer... me.

I'd been blogging and vlogging on events in and around Haxford for a good number of years now, and while I didn't consider myself a professional journalist, it was largely the same business as Lizzie's. Private investigation was another area where we were similar. Indeed, I probably had to be a little tougher than her. And yet, in all that time, no matter what aspect of my calling, I had never named and shamed anyone in public. That, as far as I was concerned, was the difference between her and me, and as I sat there, wallowing in a cocktail of self-pity and fury, I vowed that by hook or by crook I would make her pay... and James Langdon... and Heath Mottershaw... and anyone else I could think of.

It was all very well coming to such a decision, but how? I would need help. I would need someone to do what we Haxforders usually found so easy... open their mouths and tell the story.

Who saw me and reported me to the police? Who told Lizzie Finister? Why did Heath Mottershaw lie about our bland conversation(s) on

Friday night? And the most important question of all, who really murdered Katya Watkins?

The prospect of securing that help was more difficult. I could usually rely on Mandy, but she would be less forthcoming in this instance. Simon would not be allowed anywhere near the case, and although I had other friends at the police station, none of them would risk their careers to help me. I had to face it. I was on my own.

I looked around as much of the market hall as I could see from Terry's stall and everywhere screamed Christmas. Decorations hanging from the girders above, tinsel and fairy lights augmenting the stall displays, a large tree just inside the main entrance; Christmas, Christmas, Christmas. Shoppers were handing over money as if it was going out of fashion and they wanted rid of it quickly. They passed by, carrying bags laden with purchases, gift wrap, more tinsel, and what did I have? Thanks to my idiotic idea of getting Barry Snodgrass in, nothing.

Self-pity threatened to overtake me again, and I stiffened myself against it. Christmas didn't matter, I decided. Thanks to the Haxford police, Lizzie Finister and James Langdon my Christmas was in tatters along with my reputation.

But not, it seemed, with everyone.

My teacake finished, I was sipping the last of my tea when Olivia, Eric's gormless daughter, came hurrying towards me, and as she drew closer, I could see tears streaming down her cheeks.

"It's not true, is it, Mrs Capper. You've not been fired have you?"

I was so surprised by her appearance and the question that it took a few seconds for me to realise that she had got my name right. I don't think she'd ever done that before.

"I'm afraid it's true, Olivia."

As I said it she began to weep, her body racked with sobs through which she said, "It's not fair."

I signalled Terry to bring a cup of tea for her, and while we waited, I reached across the table and patted her hand. "I'll be all right, Olivia. I have other fish to fry than Radio Haxford."

She sniffed back her tears. "I didn't know you could fry Radio Haxford. Is it like fish or something, named after Dad's station?"

I chuckled. "No, love. I mean I have other ways of making a living."

"But it's not fair," she cried, and began to weep again. "You're the only one who's ever nice to me. Even when I get your name wrong, you're nice to me. That… that Reggie, he's always calling me a blunder head—" (I assumed she meant dunderhead) "— and even Dad loses his rag with me now and then, especially when I get his tea without sugar. He likes sugar." Her pretty features twisted into a mask of anger. "It's all his fault, isn't it? That Heap Bottleshore."

My sympathy waned and my senses came to full alert. "You mean Heath Mottershaw. But it's not really anything to do with him, love."

"Yes, but he came into the studio first thing Saturday morning ranting that there was no way he'd sit through an interview with a killer, and when Dad asked him what he was talking about, he said

159

you'd killed that woman from CutCost, that Catcher Watson."

"And what did your dad say to that?"

"He told Bottyshaw that he was talking rubbish, but Botty demanded to speak to Mr Langdon. Dad was in there ages with them. When he came out, he told me I wasn't to say nothing to you on account of how Mr Langdon wanted to see you this morning." Tears streamed down her cheeks. "I didn't know he was going to sack you, Justine, or I'd have rung you and told you."

I took her hand again. "It's not your fault, Olivia. Now drink your tea and calm down. There's nothing to stop us meeting for chat now and then is there?"

Actually, there was a stumbling block to our meeting now and then. She had the brains of a dormouse. That aside, she was a sweet girl with no trace of malice in her.

Contrary to my empathy for her, was building anger. Mottershaw was at Radio Haxford on Saturday morning. How did he know I'd been accused of murdering Katya Watkins? There were only two possibilities. He told the police or he knew the person who told the police and they'd passed the tale on.

If nothing else, Olivia's visit to Terry's told me where I had to go next. To the police station (again) and from there to Motty's Motors and if necessary to see Adele Mottershaw again.

First, however, I had to encourage Olivia to go back to work.

"Won't your dad be worried about where you

are?"

Her tears had dried up. "No. I came out for the morning brews, but he was upstairs with Mr Langdon when I left. He was really angry."

"Who? Mr Langdon?"

"No. Dad. He was really annoyed that you'd been fired."

"Well, I hope he doesn't put his own job on the line for my sake."

"Oh, he won't do that, Pristine, but he will say what he thinks. He allus does."

"Good. I'm pleased to hear it." I gathered my belongings. "You get on with collecting the morning teas and coffees, Olivia, and don't you worry about me. I'll be all right."

"But what will you do?"

I smiled slyly. "Hang some people out to dry, the police, a certain reporter named Finister and some of the Haxford Larpers." Now I beamed on her. "And I have you to thank for that."

Chapter Fourteen

The biggest problem facing anyone entering Haxford police station was Sergeant Vic Hillman. And I do mean big. He stood about six feet six and was built like a World War Two battle tank.

A tad older than me, we were probationers together and he never liked me. Mind, it was mostly because I gave him his nickname, Minx. Dennis told me it was model of car which Hillman used to make, and it was appropriate if only because Vic was so big that he could be anything but a Minx.

But no matter how big he was, he posed no threat to me; not in the mood I was in.

"Get out, Capper," he ordered when I walked into the station.

"Get Mandy Hiscoe or Paddy Quinn out here now."

"Are you deaf or just daft?"

"I might say the same about you. Mandy or Paddy. Now, or I call my lawyer."

"They're busy."

"Then tell them to un-busy themselves and get out here."

"For the last time, get out before I throw you out."

By now I was losing the plot. "Get one of them

out here, Minx, because if you don't, my next call is to the IOPC. Now move it."

It was a silly threat, but it did the trick. The police don't like the idea of the IOPC (Independent Office for Police Conduct) paying a visit. Hillman picked up the phone, muttered into it and put the receiver down. Taking up his pen, he used it as a pointer and directed me to the benches just inside the door. "Wait there… And don't call me Minx."

It didn't take long for a furious Paddy Quinn to appear. "What the hell do you want, Christine?"

"A serious chat… in private."

"About what?"

"I said, in private."

"Just get it said and get out."

"All right." I raised my voice. "I want to know how Heath Mottershaw knew I'd been questioned before that bag, Finister, plastered it all over the front of the Haxford Recorder."

It worked. Paddy flushed bright crimson. "I don't know what you're talking about."

"The Recorder ran the story, naming me, at about two o'clock Saturday afternoon. They were outside my door by three. Mottershaw was at Radio Haxford first thing Saturday morning, refusing to be interviewed by a killer: me. Now how did he know? There's only one answer, isn't there? One of your loudmouths told him. Now are you going to explain it to me, or do I really get in touch with the IOPC?"

Paddy had never been one to shirk a confrontation, but by now, we were attracting the attention of uniformed officers and a couple of members of the public.

163

"Come on through. We'll talk in private." He turned to Hillman. "Vic, give us an interview room and tell Mandy to meet us there."

"Number one, sir."

Paddy led the way into the station and to interview room #1 where he ordered tea, and we waited in silence for Mandy to appear. When she turned up and sat alongside him it was with a face set in the same grim mood as mine and Paddy's. Tea arrived, and Paddy asked me to run through my allegation again for Mandy's sake.

Paddy looked to Mandy and she shrugged. "I can't explain it, Chrissy, but I can assure you that the information did not come from anyone in this station. Hell, you know us. We're red hot on discipline, and especially officers keeping their mouths shut."

"In that case, you leave me with only one conclusion. Heath Mottershaw was the witness who saw me murder Katya Watkins... allegedly."

It was Paddy who answered this time. "We can't discuss that with you, and you know we can't."

"But you're not denying it. Fair enough. I'll confront him myself." I half rose.

"Hold on," Mandy urged, and as I took my seat again, she went into an urgent, whispered conversation with her boss. At length, she faced me again and announced. "All right, you win. We can deny it. We're not going to tell you who the witness was, but we can tell you it wasn't Heath Mottershaw."

"But it has to be someone close to him, and

what price that someone was the person who really murdered Katya?"

"At this moment in time," Paddy said, "you are the only suspect we have."

I clucked. "You know, Paddy, we rarely see eye to eye on anything, but I always respected your ability as a detective. Now I'm beginning to have my doubts. I did not kill Katya Watkins and you know damn well I didn't."

"We're acting on information received."

"Despite the presence of other people who might want to shuffle her off?"

That caught them on the hop.

"Who?" Mandy demanded.

"Adele Mottershaw for one. Jo Petheridge for another. Possibly Roger Trippet, because there were rumours about him and Katya. For all I know, Mottershaw himself might have wanted to see the back of her. Aidan Compton, the assistant manager at CutCost, didn't get on too well with her."

"Compton wasn't at the ball on Friday night."

"Officially," I said.

Paddy frowned. "Come again."

"I said Compton wasn't there officially, but be honest, security there was a joke. He could have sneaked in past those nurks. Reggie Monk did. As far as I was aware, he wasn't officially invited. Ignoring that, talking about Katya, I've never found anyone who had a good word to say about her. She was a class one, bad-tempered mouthpiece and the marquee could have been full of people happy to see the back of her."

"You were seen."

165

"I was not seen because I didn't do it," I retorted to Paddy's allegation. "For god's sake, her knickers were thrown off to one side. She was doing what comes naturally with some bloke, and if your medical examiner is right and that's where she was killed, then the killer was more than likely the man who gave her a good ... you know."

"We don't know that for sure," Paddy objected. "You could have yanked her pants off after killing her to make it look that way."

I switched tack. "What does the pathologist have to say about her death?"

"Nothing," Mandy confessed. "We haven't had the report yet."

"All right, what about forensics? Have they found any trace of me other than the bits after her body was discovered?"

"Not yet but you're an ex-cop. You're not daft when it comes to hiding the signs."

"But you're doing a passable impression of daft."

Paddy switched modes and went into bargaining. "Christine, give us an alibi. Anything that'll help us clear your name."

I had to think about that. "Time," I said. "Do you have a time of death?"

The inspector shrugged. "Sometime between nine-fifteen and ten o'clock, which was when her body was discovered."

I latched onto a glimmer of hope. "I was talking to Heath Mottershaw at about half past nine, and at that time, Katya was still alive and talking to Kim Aspinall. I was on my way to rescue Kim when

Mottershaw intercepted me."

Paddy was suddenly alert and I sensed victory coming my way. "What? Why the hell didn't you say so sooner?"

"Because you never talked about the time of death, did you? You simply relied on this lying witness."

"Or mistaken witness," Mandy put in.

I sneered. "My eye."

She tried to defend their actions. "To get it right, we didn't have an estimated time of death in the early hours of Saturday. We didn't get that until yesterday."

Paddy chewed his lip. "We still only have your word for this, Chrissy." He faced Mandy. "We need to get onto Aspinall and see if we can confirm it." He switched his attention to me. "So you were talking to Mottershaw at half nine. And after that?"

"I was with Kim and Jo Petheridge. Kim wandered off and the next thing Jo and I knew was the scream from the toilets at about ten."

Was that true? Was I still with Jo when that happened? I couldn't really remember.

Regardless of that, Mandy shot it down right away. "It's not enough. You still had a small window of opportunity, Chrissy. It might be thin, but it's there."

"All right, I'll just have to confront Mottershaw over this morning's revelations." Again, I half rose, then changed my mind. "What about the business with Finister at our house?"

It was Mandy who shrugged this time. "Nothing we can do about it unless she drops the charges."

This time, I did get up. "She'll drop them. Either that, or I'll shame her and her ilk to hell."

Paddy, too, rose. "You know the script, Christine. If you learn anything you must bring it to us."

"And I will. One last thing. When you clear my name, will you go public on it?"

He actually smiled. "Count on it."

***

Motty's Motors was a bog-standard used car lot on Huddersfield Road half a mile further out than CutCost and on the outskirts of town. A dog rough patch of ground with a number of second hand cars, all facing the road, each with its own price tag, anything from £599 for an ageing Toyota to £4500 for a newer, but still out of date Vauxhall. All up, I calculated he had about twenty vehicles on sale, and he had just one young couple wandering around, checking the cars.

But he didn't want my company, and he made that clear the moment I pulled up outside the lot and walked towards him.

"I sold that piece of crap to your old man months ago. I don't want it back."

"And I don't want to sell it. I want to sell you… down the river."

He delivered a puzzled glower. "You're not making any sense, woman. Now clear off before I call the cops."

"Your wife says you're strapped for cash for

this dump," I gestured around me, "so save yourself the cost of the call. Paddy Quinn and Mandy Hiscoe will be here before the morning's out."

He took out his mobile and held it up for me to see. "Want me to talk to Langdon, then?"

"Go ahead," I invited. "You did that on Saturday morning, didn't you? Told him straight that you didn't want to be interviewed by a woman suspected of murder."

"I made my feelings plain on the matter."

"As a result of which, I got fired this morning. So go ahead and call Langdon."

By now, the young couple had lost interest in the cars and were focussed on the argument. Mottershaw looked from me to them and back again as I pressed home my attack.

"You shot yourself in the foot, Theah the Mighty Mouth. You announced that I was a murder suspect before anyone other than me and the police knew about it. I didn't tell you, I'm assured the police didn't, so who did? My guess is, no one. You accused me for one reason only. Because you did it. You were first at the scene when Katya was found. I even stopped you moving her. What were you going to do? Try to hide the evidence?"

His face ran a gamut of expressions from alarm to outright horror, and back to anger. He took a threatening pace towards me.

"Stop." I held up my hand to forestall him. "Come any closer and Theah the Big Gob will learn just how vicious Christine the Crazy Catwoman can be."

He stopped and his anger rose again. "I never

touched her."

"Then how did you know I was suspected? How did you know I was hauled into the police station at three in the morning?"

"I didn't." All of a sudden there was a note of pleading in his voice.

"You're a second-hand car salesman and I'd expect you to be a better liar than that. How did you know?"

"It was..." He looked frantic, as if he was searching for an excuse. "It was... you. Yes. That's it. It was you. You said you knew the signs of murder and robbery. I thought that was rubbish so I thought you'd done it."

"And you told the police that?"

"Well, er, no. I didn't."

I let out a frustrated sigh. "I was a police officer, and they trained us to recognise bullplop, and you're feeding me nothing but. Quite honestly, as a salesman, you're giving me so much flannel that you couldn't sell me a spare wheel never mind a car."

"Yes but—"

"You suspected I'd shuffled Katya Watkins off her mortal coil and you didn't tell the police that but you felt so strongly about it that you ran to James Langdon with the story? If I choose to be charitable and assume that you didn't kill her, who told you it was me?"

"Bugger off. Y'hear me? Just get lost. I've nowt to say to you."

I glanced along the road and spotted a familiar Vauxhall headed towards us. "Fair enough. Just so you know, this is Mandy Hiscoe's car, and she'll be taking you in for questioning, and while they're giving you the third degree down the cop shop, I'll have a word or five with your missus."

The young couple were transfixed by the scene as Mandy pulled in behind my car, and climbed out with Sonny Scott as backup. Mottershaw was transfixed, too, but his was more fear than rabid interest.

Mandy nodded to me. "Learned anything?"

"Yes. I've learned he's such a rubbish liar, he should be in politics. It's no wonder he's not selling any cars."

She smiled and then concentrated on the worried salesmen. "Mr Mottershaw, we're taking you in on suspicion of withholding evidence possibly pertinent to a serious crime. I must caution you—"

"I've a business to run."

"Tell the truth when we get to the station and you'll be back here in a couple of hours," Mandy told him, and went into her caution again.

The young couple came to me. "What about us?" the lad asked. "We wanted a car off him."

"I'm sorry, loves, but listen. Do yourself a favour and nip over to Haxford Fixers. They're in Haxford Mill. Ask for Dennis and tell him Christine sent you."

"He'll do us a deal, will he?" the blonde girlfriend asked.

"Better than Motty ever would, and I know Dennis well. He's a top drawer mechanic. Whatever you buy off him, you can guarantee it's the best." I watched Sonny escort Mottershaw to the car, then I beamed on the couple again. "In fact, I'm going that way. I can give you a lift if you like."

The young man gave me a wan smile. "Er, kind of you, but, er no. We'll make our own way there. Thanks." And with that they scurried off.

I think the exchange with Mottershaw had unnerved them, and I doubted that Dennis and his pals would see them.

I told Mottershaw I would be going to see his wife, but I was on the wrong side of town, and CutCost was actually nearer. Adele Mottershaw could wait; Aidan Compton was my next target.

I did a U-turn, cutting across a van coming from Huddersfield, and he gave me several flashes... of angry headlights, I hasten to add, and when I moved over to the right hand lane to turn into CutCost, he gave me a blast on the horn and a threatening fist as he passed on his way into Haxford.

I saw it as an omen. I doubted that Aidan would welcome me with open arms, unless those arms were field cannon. Regardless, I had to speak to him. I didn't care what Mandy and Paddy said, he could well have been there at the Christmas Ball.

The first problem was getting to see him, I waited at the customer service desk, which doubled up as the lottery and tobacco kiosk, until one of the attendants approached me. She rang him and got a flat, 'no'.

When she passed the message on, I kept my voice down. "Tell him if he doesn't speak to me, he'll be talking to DI Quinn in about twenty minutes."

She passed the message on and a couple of minutes later, Aidan hurried out of his office, a face like thunder, and railed into me. "Mrs Capper, I'm a busy man and I don't take kindly—"

"This would be better in private, Aidan."

"You are suspected of—"

"Not any longer, I'm not," I lied. "The police will be making the announcement soon and your name has been mentioned. I thought if you spoke to me, I could clear you before they get here."

That stopped him dead. He spent a few seconds thinking about it, and then said, "Come through to my office."

His office was a windowless cubbyhole not much larger than our bathroom. In fact, take out the bath, shower and toilet and our bathroom might be bigger. It was filled with the usual paraphernalia of such a place... his office, I mean, not our bathroom. Box files ranged on shelves, a computer monitor up and running, and a desk cluttered with bits of paper almost burying the telephone.

"So, Mrs Capper, what can I do for you?"

"You were at the Christmas Festival Ball on Friday night. I saw you dressed as Napoleon."

I thought I might as well take a leaf from Paddy Quinn's book and accuse rather than ask, but it backfired right away.

"I'm afraid not. I was working here until ten, and I got home about half past. My wife will verify that. I don't know who you saw, Christine, but it wasn't me."

"Oh. My apologies." I chuckled. "I really

should get my eyes tested." I hummed and aahed for a moment. "Katya. I know I had a couple of spats with her, but the word is she was like that with everyone."

His face became grave. "One should not speak ill of the dead, but I'm afraid that's true. She needed to work on her people skills, but she was top notch at her job."

"Joanne Petheridge doesn't think so. Katya accused her of shoplifting."

His features darkened further. "I remember the incident, and we did discipline Katya for it. Not only her but the security guard too, and we did our best to placate Mrs Petheridge... to little avail, I'm afraid. We don't see her very often these days, and the last time I spoke to her, she said, and I quote, if she ever laid eyes on Katya again, she would throttle her."

My heart leapt. Hadn't I mentioned Jo to Paddy and Mandy earlier, but she couldn't have murdered Katya... could she? She was with me at the time. Or was she?

"Thanks, Aidan. You've given me a bit of a lead if nothing else."

Chapter Fifteen

Aidan's words concerning Jo made me stop and think. She freely admitted that she didn't like Katya, and her Cleopatra outfit did have some sort of chain around the crown thing she was wearing. Was it possible that this witness who spoke to the police mistook me for Jo? We were dressed in a similar manner, and with the best will in the world, I was slightly better known than her; someone it would be easier to put a name to.

How to approach the prospect. I'd only known her a week and I already considered her a friend, so it would need a softly, softly approach. First, however, I would have to rack my brain to work out whether Jo was with me at the time Katya's body was discovered, or whether she really had a window of opportunity sufficient to let her throttle the woman.

I'd originally planned to call on Adele Mottershaw, but this new information forced a change of plan, and I made for home instead, to be greeted by a surly Cappy the Cat who was obviously starving to death and bursting to pay a call on the Timminses.

There are techniques for jogging your memory, but frankly I'd never found any need of them, and when I tried them now, they didn't work, mainly because Friday evening was not much more than a fog in my head.

I was flitting about online and I saw a photograph of Elvis Presley, and it reminded me of Reggie Monk's costume on Friday night. That was one hundred percent after I spoke to Jo about her experience of Katya Watkins. Beyond Reggie, I recalled speaking to young Barry – Barnes, not Snodgrass – Terry Shakespeare, our self-important mayor, and his wife, and it was only after speaking to them for a minute or two that I went in search of Jo to call it a night, and that was when the alert went up.

OMG. She wasn't with me. She did have the opportunity.

At least, assuming I was right about the way the job was done, i.e. with Katya taken off to one side, away from the toilets where they would be in shadow, Jo had the chance to do it. And it might explain why someone said they saw me committing the crime. Our costumes were not exactly alike, but they were similar, and if the witness' brain was fogged by alcohol (like mine) it would be easy to mistake Jo for me. And if the witness' brain was not fogged by alcohol, what was he/she doing at the ball in the first place?

I ordered my mind to focus on ways and means of approaching Jo on the matter. I instantly dismissed the Dennis Capper tactic of, "Right, lass, did you top the Watkins bag on Friday night?" True, it had the merit of simplicity, but it was not conducive to a civilised response or subsequent debate.

It was a path of eggshells, threatening what I'd hoped would be a burgeoning friendship.

One of the big problems I faced as a private eye was my solitariness. That's an appalling word, but what I mean is the manner in which I worked alone. For instance, Holmes had his Watson, Poirot his Hastings, Wimsey had Bunter, and a chap I met some years ago, Joe Murray, Chair of the Sanford 3rd Age Club and an amateur sleuth, had his girlfriends, Sheila Riley and Brenda Jump. These people acted as sounding boards, men (women in the case of Murray) upon whom they could test theories, take feedback, people who would offer their own ideas which, right or wrong, would prompt the detective in different ways.

Who did I have? Dennis? His idea of advice would be to say something like, "That reminds me of this motor I worked on where I was sure the track rod ends had gone…"

I worked alone. Granted, there was Kim at the library but she wasn't the brightest spark in the universe, and I had Mandy, but as a serving police officer she was obliged to remain tight-lipped when it came to giving out information.

A week and a bit after first meeting Jo, I had warmed to her and I hoped that we would become close enough friends for her to act as my sounding board. One phone call asking whether she murdered Katya Watkins would be enough to ensure the promise never materialised.

On the other hand, Katya Watkins deserved justice… well, I say deserved, but what I really mean is we could not allow people to rub out others purely because they didn't like them. If such was the case, I would turn Haxford into a ghost town overnight, and it was certain that I'd be on a good number of hit lists.

Someone had to grasp the nettle, bite the bullet.

Why is it when we're facing that kind of dilemma, all we can come up with are old clichés?

I picked up my phone and with a noticeably trembling finger, hit the icon for Jo.

She answered right away, bright as... I was going to say a button, but that would be another cliché. She was chirpy and friendly, and I had to wonder how long that would last.

"Hi, Chrissy. Oh, I read about your problems in the Recorder. How awful for you. They don't really suspect you, do they?"

I kept my tone even and as friendly as I could. "Not really, but someone said they'd seen me, so the police had no option but to question me."

"And what about that Finister woman? Did you punch her?"

"I'm afraid so."

"She's earned it. I've read some of her pieces and scurrilous doesn't begin to cover it."

"Yes, well, it's created an unholy mess for a lot of people, not least me... and you."

The first sign of her attitude deteriorating came after a short pause. "Me?"

I felt like I was walking through a minefield as I explained. "I had a small window of opportunity to commit the crime, and I'm sorry, Jo, but so did you."

178

I recalled the way she told me she'd confronted teenagers when they took the mickey with her name, and for a brief moment I felt sorry for them. "You seriously imagine that I killed Watkins?"

"That's not what I'm saying—"

She snapped completely. "Well that's what it sounds like. Do me a favour, Christine. Get off the line, and if you ever ring me again it'll be too soon."

And with that she cut the call.

My heart sank. It was exactly as I feared. Worse, it merely shored up my suspicions. Anger, I could understand. Wasn't I angry when Mandy came to take me in for questioning? But such outrage? It all shouted bluff to me. From being a distant suspect, Jo was suddenly front and centre.

Things didn't get any better when I rang Mandy to let her know what had happened.

"It wasn't her, Chrissy. The chain on her crown thing is nothing like the right kind, and anyway we have her on a shedload of pictures before, during and after the event, and we don't think she had the opportunity. The same, by the way, goes for you, so I think we're well on the way to clearing you."

"But you still don't have a clue?"

"Nope. Not at this point, but cheer up. We'll get there. I'm sure we will."

Oh dear. What kind of mess had I got myself into this time? In a desperate effort to clear my name, I was accusing everyone at the ball. Who next? Terry Shakespeare? Mind you, if anyone deserved that kind of accusation it was Terry Shakespeare.

Things would only get worse when Dennis

came home just before seven o'clock, carrying a copy of the Haxford Recorder and wearing a face like a wet weekend in Withernsea, and if you've ever been to Withernsea during a wet weekend, then you know precisely what I mean.

He started his usual opening gambit. "Hey up, lass. What's for tea?"

I scowled back. "Whatever I can be bothered throwing in the microwave."

"Like that, is it? fair enough." He sat at the table. "Any danger of a pot of tea? And you'd better make one for yourself. You'll need it."

I was halfway to the freezer when he said it. I stopped and looked back. He had laid the Recorder out on the table, front page uppermost and it was dominated by a large photograph. From my point of view, it was upside down, but I could still make out the features of Lizzie Finister.

"You make us some tea," I told him as I marched back to the table and snatched the newspaper from under his elbows.

The moment I looked at the photograph, my blood began to boil. The injury to her lip, courtesy my knuckles was there, but her right eye was also blackened, and that had nothing to do with me.

But according to the text, it did.

REPORTER ASSAULTED FOR DOING HER JOB, screamed the headline.

The Recorder's chief crime reporter, Lizzie Finister suffered a vicious assault at the hands of local celebrity, Christine Capper on Saturday afternoon, leaving her with a split lip and a black eye.

180

Interviewed by a staff reporter, Ms Finister, one of our longest serving colleagues, had this to say. "I was following up the reports of Mrs Capper's arrest after the murder of Katya Watkins on Friday night. She emerged from her house, marched straight up to the gate where I and a number of other reporters were waiting, and without warning, she punched me first in the mouth and then in the eye. Her husband, Dennis Capper, then dragged her back into the house."

Mrs Capper never said a word so there is no explanation of the attack, but the theory is that Lizzie was the first to release her name after her arrest.

Lizzie was present at the Christmas Festival Ball on Friday evening, and standing by journalistic principles, she has refused to name the source of her information regarding Mrs Capper's arrest.

See editorial: page 5.

Hands shaking with fury, I turned to the editorial and fumed some more.

THE RECORDER SAYS:

It's high time the police clamped down on violence in this town. The cowardly attack on Lizzie Finister was unprovoked and unwarranted, but as is widely known, Christine Capper, blogger, vlogger, private eye, and part time radio presenter, is also an ex-police officer.

And that gives her the right to assault a woman simply doing her job? Here at the Recorder...

I threw the paper to one side. I could not read any further.

Dennis picked it up, dropped a beaker of tea in

front of me, and sat opposite. My hands were still shaking when I picked up the beaker to take a (non) calming sip of tea.

"Soon as I saw it I rang him in charge," Dennis said. "Him as was trying to get your pants off afore you met me."

"Ian Noiland. I dated him, Dennis, and he did not try to get my knickers off... Well, he might have tried, but he didn't actually get there." I put some steel into my voice. "Mark my words, by the time I've done with him tomorrow, he'll be hiding his bruises behind his underpants."

"Don't talk so blinking daft, woman. You're in enough trouble as it is. Anyroad, I told him, I said, no way did my missus black that cow's eye. I know, cos I were there. That picture's been faked."

"And how did he react?"

"He told me to get stuffed."

"I've a good mind to go down there tomorrow morning."

"No you don't. After I'd done with him, I rang our Simon, and he said he'd take it up with Mandy Hiscoe."

That perked me up a little. "Right. Dennis, be a love and get one of those frozen minced beef hotpots out of the freezer. Punch through the plastic covering with a fork and put it in the microwave for four minutes. I should be through talking to Mandy by then, and I'll take over."

While he set about the job, I took out my smartphone and rang my favourite detective.

"Is it about the Recorder?"

"What else. Mandy, they're lying. I didn't—"

182

"We know."

"—punch her in… Pardon me?"

"I said we know. When Simon told me, I had a look at the paper, and then called Sonny Scott in. He came out to your place on Saturday, remember. He told us right away that Lizzie didn't look like that when he saw her. Paddy was going down there to speak to Noiland before he signed off. Now, I need you to do us a favour, Chrissy. Leave it to us. Please."

"I don't know. I know Noiland well, and he deserves a mouthful. She's always been economical with the truth, but I thought better of him. And vicious assault? All I did was punch her in the gob, but if I get my hands on her she'll soon learn what a vicious assault is really like."

"Don't do it, Chrissy. Charges could follow from this, so please, leave it to us."

I hesitated again, then capitulated. "All right."

Chapter Sixteen

Monday was the absolute nadir of the entire fiasco. In the space of a single day, I lost almost everything, including my part time job and my temper more than a time or two.

Tuesday started badly when I tuned into Radio Haxford and learned that my 11 o'clock agony aunt slot would be filled by no less a cow than Lizzie Finister. It made sense in a perverted sort of way. She was the station's agony aunt before me, but she was sacked for political bias. But she had the experience and at such short notice, she was the obvious choice. That she still sported a fat lip, courtesy my knuckles, was irrelevant. It might give her a bit of a lisp but it was invisible on radio

When I got out of bed at eight on Tuesday morning, I vowed that I would turn this round, and half an hour later, I got the first uplift when Mandy rang me.

"Paddy'll be on the local news at nine, Chrissy, both TV and radio, and he'll formally clear you of any suspicion. And this time, he will name you and he'll hit out at the Recorder over that photograph and for printing your name in the first place."

"But you won't drop the assault charge."

"Sorry, kiddo, but that's up to Lizzie Finister,

not us. Fake picture or not, you did thump her, and the law won't take account of her deserving it."

"But I'm clean and green with regard to Katya Watkins?"

"Spot on. Fact is, the chain on your handbag just didn't match the scarring on Katya's neck, and when we spoke to Motty yesterday, he confirmed that he was yattering with you around the time she was murdered. But before you get out of your pram, he wasn't the one who fingered you, and that timing clears him as much as it does you. True, you both still had a tiny window of opportunity, but we don't think so in either case."

"Did he tell you who told him I was a suspect?"

"He claims he overheard someone talking to Lizzie Finister but he couldn't identify the person in question."

"Couldn't or wouldn't?"

"Take your pick."

"All right. What about my toga costume? I need to take it back to the hire shop."

"You can pick it up when you're ready."

"I'll be down later. When I've watched Paddy."

That got the day off to a good start and it got better when I switched on the TV just before nine, in time to catch Paddy's moment of glory on the local news.

"After taking into account forensic evidence, we can now say that Mrs Christine Capper, who was questioned as a suspect in the murder of Katya Watkins, is now cleared of any involvement or suspicion. A former police officer based in Haxford, Mrs Capper was named, without our agreement or consent, in the Haxford Recorder as a suspect on Saturday, causing a great deal of distress for her and her family. We are certain that the leak did not come from within Haxford police station, and after fruitless discussions with Ian Noiland, the managing editor at the Recorder, who refused to divulge the source of this information, we are now formulating a report to the Press Complaints Commission. As far as we are concerned, Mrs Capper was only one of a number of people questioned on this crime, and yet her name was the only one leaked, and it should not have been, at least until such times as charges were prepared." Paddy paused and held up the previous evening's Recorder. "Furthermore, the photograph adorning the front page of last night's Haxford Recorder is an obvious fake. Mrs Capper admitted the assault on Ms Finister, but one of our officers interviewed the reporter shortly after the event, and while she had a slight injury to her lip, there was no damage to her eyes. The only conclusion we can reach is that the photograph was faked with the use of cosmetic makeup. I have discussed these issues with Mr Noiland, the managing editor, and made it clear that charges could follow, and in addition, should Mrs Capper elect to sue the Haxford Recorder, she will have the support of the West Yorkshire police."

Paddy I love you.

That was the first, absurd thought which ran through my mind as the waiting crowd of press wolves bombarded him with questions on who might have killed Katya.

He did have a point. I could sue the Recorder

but they never actually accused me of the crime and I suspected that the compensation would be minimal. Punching Lizzie Finister in the mouth was a genuine crime, and the tribunal would take that into account, and I had no doubt that Radio Haxford would say it was clouting Lizzie which led to my dismissal. The Recorder could face the courts for faking the photograph, but I knew Ian Noiland well. He would never be party to such a blatant scam. He would disclaim responsibility and blame Lizzie, and quite honestly, I couldn't think of a finer pair of narrow shoulders to hang the blame on than hers.

Still and all, I was on the up and after watching Paddy, I moved to the bedroom to dress for the day, mentally listing the calls I had to make and the people I had to see, and after the news, they were people from whom I would not take no for an answer.

As I was primping my hair in front of the wardrobe mirror, I recalled the missing earring, and made a mental note to check the toga when I got it back from Mandy. From there I'd return it to Wilma Elmond. That would be an argument, in its own right. Technically the garment was 24 hours late, but that wasn't my fault and I would not pay for it.

Clad in jogging pants, a thick jumper, and getting my winter coat ready, carrying the previous evening's Recorder (I had plans for that) I was about to leave the house just before ten, when the mobile rang. Eric Reitman. I cut it off, and seconds later, I got a text from him.

Please answer, Chrissy. It's urgent.

So when it rang again, I made the connection.

"Eric, I thought I made it clear yesterday that I'm through with Radio Haxford."

"You did, but after listening to Detective Inspector Quinn this morning, I was in with Langdon, and things might be changing. I'm tied up until noon when Reggie goes off air. Could you meet me at Terry's at, say, quarter past?"

"So you can tell me how you've chickened out like you did during the Prater affair? I don't think so."

"I did not chicken out during the Prater affair, and I don't know where you got that idea from. Please, Chrissy, this is important. Especially for you."

I sighed. "All right. I'll be at Terry's for quarter past twelve."

Eric had done so much for me during my time at Radio Haxford that it was only fair to listen to what he had to say, but during the Prater affair, he was hauled before Langdon and suffered a reading of the riot act, after which he capitulated. To be scrupulously fair, both he and I were arrested during that case, and I don't mean questioned as suspects, but arrested and charged for withholding evidence possibly prejudicial to an ongoing investigation. As it turned out, the police let us both go with a caution.

By toeing the line, Eric came to my rescue then, salvaging the agony aunt spot on my behalf, but the situation this time was different. It involved only me, not him, and I couldn't imagine what he had to tell me. After the acrimonious interlude with Langdon, I also couldn't see the big boss backing down, and I certainly wouldn't.

It was quarter past ten when I finally climbed into the car and under a surly stare from Cappy the Cat, set off for town.

First port of call, the police station to collect my belongings, and then the costume hire place to argue the toss with Wilma, then the meeting with Eric, and from there... Adele Mottershaw, Heath Mottershaw, Roger Trippet, Jo Petheridge, and anyone else I could think of who deserved the rough edge of my tongue. Somewhere along the line, I needed a few Christmas decs, too. There was less than a week to the big feast and I wanted that house looking something like.

Mandy was ready for me. The toga and handbag were still wrapped in evidence bags on her desk when I sat with her.

She handed over my missing stirrup hoop earring. "We found this trapped in the folds of the toga. Since Katya was still wearing both of hers, we figured it belonged to you. And yes, we did test it for traces, but there's only you on it.

"I was wondering where it got to and I eventually guessed it was in the toga. The clasp is a bit weak and it's forever falling out." I dropped it in my pocket. "So, I'm officially cleared of all suspicion? At least that's what Paddy said on the telly."

She nodded and explained, "There were traces of Katya on the toga, but they were inconsequential, and probably came about when you checked her to see if she was still alive. You admitted as much, and since Motty confirmed it, we can eliminate you

189

completely from the inquiry. All that is over and above the scarring on her neck which didn't match the chain on your handbag. Whoever killed her used a much thicker chain."

"A rope chain, Paddy said, didn't he?"

"It's the only chain he knows, aside from the one you used to pull in lavatories. It's actually thicker and stronger than an ornamental rope chain. More like... like... do you remember the old-fashioned choke chains they used to get for dogs?"

"Old-fashioned nothing. The pet stall in the market hall still sells them. I've often thought of buying one for Cappy the Cat, but that little sod would only find a way of wriggling out of it."

Mandy was not interested in the antics of my moody moggie. "They still sell them? Maybe I should make a few inquiries. According to our forensic bods, this was highly polished, so it could be new."

"It could also belong to some barmpot who likes to see his German Shepherd prim and proper when he takes it walkies."

She changed the subject. "So where are you up to?"

I gave her a detailed list of my potential calls, and when I mentioned Wilma Elmond and the possible bill for a late return, she laughed.

"Pointless sending that cranky old sow here. We won't pay her."

"And I won't either so she's likely to be even crankier."

From the police station, my next port of call was Haxford Costume Hire, but before I got there, a tiny bell rang in the back of my mind, so I went back to my car first, settled into the driving seat, and rang Jo.

She cut the call and a few seconds later, I got a text. "I've nothing to say to you."

I recalled Eric's trick earlier, and I texted back. *Please Jo, answer the phone. I'm sorry about yesterday, but I need to speak to you urgently.*

After sending it off, I rang again, and for the second time she cut me off, so I rang a third time, and this time, probably having read the text, she answered.

"What do you want, Christine? Didn't you say enough yesterday?"

"I was under severe stress, Jo, and you're not the only one I upset. I'm sorry, but as I said, you had small window of opportunity. Anyway, I've been officially cleared—"

"Good. Enjoy your new-found innocence. Goodbye."

"No. Wait…"

Too late. She ended the call again.

I don't know where the term 'flogging a dead horse' came from but I knew what it meant, and I wasn't about to ring her again. Not just yet.

Instead, I tucked the earring back into the folds of the toga, left the car and made my way through the chilly streets to Wilma Elmond's place. The streets were not the only thing cold. So was she.

"Late back. I'll have to charge you for it."

I gave her a vicious smile. "You do that. I won't pay, but by all means carry on."

"You'll pay."

191

"Or what?"

For the first time she was off guard, uncertain which way to go. "I'll... I'll call the cops. Yeah. That's what I'll do. I'll bell the filth."

"I can wait, so please, go ahead," I invited before dropping into insult mode. "Tell me something, do you spend so much time helping people live in a fantasy world that you live in one too? Are you not up to snuff with the news? Katya Watkins, another of your customers judging by the costume she was wearing, was murdered on Friday night, and I was taken in for questioning on it after some prat accused me. The police kept the Aphrodite costume and I've only just got it back. You want to bill anyone, bill them, but I've already been told, unofficially of course, that they'll tell you right where you can go... and take your costumes with you. And on that note, Mrs Elmond, I'll take my leave of you."

Stiff-backed, I walked out of the shop, but I could feel her glare burning through me as I left.

Out on the street again, I checked my watch. Half past eleven. Forty-five minutes to kill before I met with Eric. Just enough time to go to Benny's Bargain Basement and pick up some Christmas trinkets.

Benny's was one of my favourites. The kind of shop which literally sold everything, and if he didn't he would get it for you in a matter of twenty-four hours. As a consequence, I came away from his High Street place at ten past twelve, carrying three bags full of Christmassy stuff (tinsel, baubles, figurines, and some fake snow) and I had to rush through the streets to the market hall in time to meet Eric. Indeed I was two minutes late but he'd already ordered tea, and he'd paid in advance for the toasted teacake he knew I would want.

From the very first time I met him, I got on well with Eric. Soft spoken, gentle with newcomers like me, encouraging, and even when he had to pull me up for one blunder or another, he did so in a constructive manner. Socially, however, he was also a notorious small-talker, a man who had to warm up before he got to the point.

He did it now. How was I, how was Dennis, how were the rest of the family, were we looking forward to Christmas, and so on.

I stood it for so long (until I finished my teacake, actually) and then cut him short.

"You asked me here, Eric, because you had... I don't know... information for me. Could we get to the point, please?"

"Yes. Sorry, Christine. You're right of course." He took a long breath, as if rehearsing his approach, sipped some tea, and then went into his announcement. "The situation is complex, but I had a frank face to face with Langdon after hearing DI Quinn on the radio. The meeting got quite heated. I didn't agree with the way he treated you, especially on the say so of people like Heath Mottershaw and Lizzie Finister. Mottershaw is a simpleton as far as I'm concerned, and the less said about Finister the better. Faking that photograph was beyond the pale, and didn't we fire her for political bias during that by-election? We dragged her back in this morning because of her prior experience, by the way. She's not been appointed. Right now, she's a stopgap and no way will she get a contract. Not if I have anything to do with it. She's there only until we can get you back behind the microphone."

I shook my head. "It won't happen, Eric. Not now, not ever. I don't need Radio Haxford."

"Please hear me out, Chrissy, and whatever you do, don't burn your bridges. Not yet. I said the meeting got heated, and at one point, Langdon threatened me with the sack. As you know, I'm not on a contract, I'm employed. Voices were raised, and in the end I told him to do what he likes, and from there, I put in a complaint to the board of governors. Reggie Monk countersigned it. We've had enough of Langdon's dictatorship, and if we can press our point strongly enough, we'll have him removed as controller."

I was pleased to hear it, but I kept the thought to myself. "It won't make any difference, Eric. Given the circumstances, I could have understood if he'd suspended me, but he didn't. He fired me and actually said that guilt and innocence made no difference."

"He said the same to me, and I pointed out that if he applied that to everyone in the studio, he could be firing people for getting parking tickets. I mean, how much grief has Reggie caused down the years, usually when he's drunk or tries to pull some married woman?" Eric fell silent for a moment. "You did punch Lizzie though, didn't you?"

"She deserved it. Naming me might not be illegal, but it's against protocol. And I have her to tackle yet. I still don't know who told her."

He drummed thoughtful fingers on the table. "Are you prepared to go public on all of this?"

"Too right, I am. I'll be preparing my vlog when I get home today."

"I'm not talking about a tuppeny-ha'penny vlog."

Eric's candour surprised and hurt me. He'd never been scathing about my vlog. Indeed, it was one of the things which persuaded him to hire me as the agony aunt in the first place.

"I'm talking television," he went on. "If I can fix it up with TVYK, would you be prepared to tell all in front of the cameras?"

That caught me on the hop. "Television? Oh, I don't know. I mean radio is one thing—"

"And you eventually got used to it."

I went on as if he had never interrupted. "But television? I'm not sure."

"You don't have to do anything dramatic. Just be yourself and tell your tale. Listen, Chrissy, I've been in this business a long time, and I've not been limited to radio. I have friends in TV. It'll only take one phone call and they'll be backing you up."

I shrank back. "All to get Langdon fired?"

"No. To get justice for you and other people who may have been put in this position. Please, Chrissy, say you'll give it a go and I'll make the call this afternoon."

I was still hesitant, but eventually I gave him a nod.

"Great. I'll speak to Gaynor Armistead this afternoon. She produces The Local View, TVYK's six o'clock magazine programme, and if I know her, you'll be on tomorrow evening's edition."

I gave him a weak smile and swallowed hard. What had I got myself into now?

Chapter Seventeen

Why was I so easy to persuade into doing things I didn't really want to do?

That was the question I asked myself as I drove out of town on Sheffield Road, making for the Mottershaws' place.

Reggie Monk had persuaded me to take up the agony aunt slot on Radio Haxford, and later, Eric talked me into other programmes, and when they went sour, Langdon persuaded me to take on the Christine Capper Interview. Eric also sweet-talked me into my first appearance before a live audience. And as if all that were not enough during that same gig, Paddy Quinn dumped the responsibility for leading the murder investigation on his behalf (on account of how we were snowed in and the police couldn't get to us).

And now, by playing on the calamity which had taken over my life, Eric had persuaded me to appear on The Local View, TVYK's early evening magazine programme, and I conceded without so much as a whimper.

Obviously I had still had time to say no. When this woman rang and it was almost certainly when, not if, I could tell her to go away, but knew I wouldn't. Why? Because television was a dream from… well, forever, really, but it only seriously took hold in my head when I started vlogging. I fancied myself as a TV reporter.

Strange, when I stopped to think about it. I recalled how nervous I was when I first went on air as Radio Haxford's agony aunt. Now I was terrified of the prospect of appearing on TV.

And this would not be first time I'd been interviewed on TV. The last time was a two-minute spot on the local news shortly after the successful outcome of the Prater case, but that was more about my uncovering what had gone on, not what had happened to me personally.

The drive out of town did give me time to think about my approach and the people I'd have to forewarn – essentially Dennis, Mandy, and Paddy. Dennis to prevent him barging in on the interview, Mandy and Paddy because they could get some flak. Although I was furious with them in the early hours of Saturday morning, they were only doing their job and I could not blame them for the fiasco which followed (unless it did turn out to be one of their officers or support staff who had named me to the Recorder). That unlikely possibility aside, culpability lay with Lizzie (anything for a story) Finister, Ian (anything plus one for a headline) Noiland, and James (I'm the king of the castle) Langdon, and assuming this producer woman didn't object, I would name all three.

I pulled up outside the Mottershaws' house, killed the engine, rang Mandy and told her of this new development.

"Go for it is all I can say," she replied, "but you

have my absolute assurance that no one at this station spoke to Finister or the Recorder."

"And I'll accept that, Mandy. Are you doing anything about that fake photograph?"

She was hesitant. "Difficult to know what we can do. We're not sure what, if any, laws she's broken. Harassment perhaps, but it's thin. Having said that, there's plenty you could do about it. Go to the Recorder, maybe with your Stephen in tow, and confront Noiland."

Stephen was my brother, a Haxford based solicitor and he was more than capable of handling civil and criminal cases. But he was also a non-starter. "Stephen and Melinda are in Tenerife until about Thursday or Friday," I explained, "and right now, I have to speak to Adele Mottershaw."

"Well, before you do, you didn't hear it from me, but she wasn't the one who fingered you."

"Good to know. Thanks, Mandy."

I cut the call, reached into my bag for my copy of the Recorder, and then climbed out of the car, locked up and marched up the path.

The moment Adele opened the door, it was a prelude to war. "What do you want?"

"Paying," I announced, "and when you've paid me, I want to know why you wasted Katya Watkins and tried to blame me."

All right, so Mandy told me it wasn't her, but after the previous three days, I was in attack mode and still determined to blame anyone.

She took a half pace forward and stopped dead when I held up the Recorder, Lizzie's picture staring out at her.

199

"Before you think about it, Adele, think again. This bitch only named me and you can see the mess I made of her. You tried to frame me."

"I didn't."

The potential threat was gone. This was a woman pleading her innocence. Exactly the effect I'd hoped for.

"Do we talk out here or in there?" I asked, pointing along the hall.

She stood back to let me in, closed the door behind us, and led the way to the kitchen. She did not offer tea, which was a blessing. I still remembered how bad it tasted.

Sitting opposite her, I made my positon clear. "You owe me for the work I did chasing up the ring, and you owe me an explanation for the way your husband declared me a killer before even that bitch, Finister knew. Seems to me there was only one way. You told him because you were the one who fingered me to the cops."

"Well you're wrong. I didn't even know he'd said anything about you." Some of her fire had returned.

"He said it to Langdon, the big boss at Radio Haxford. And he managed to get me fired. So if not you, then who?"

"I don't bloody know do I?"

"And you didn't know he was hauled into the police station yesterday?"

That hit her right between the eyes. "What?"

I nodded slowly, gravely. "They wanted to know where he got his information from, too. Course, they wouldn't bring me into their

200

confidence. Even though I've been cleared, they won't tell me what he said. So you tell me."

"Oh, for crying out loud... He tells me nothing. Not a bloody word. So I can't tell you nothing. Take it up with him."

"Don't worry, I will. Now, as for your ring, I think I know where it went. You were right. Your old man took it, but he didn't hawk it. He gave it Katya Watkins for their LARP games, and that stupid woman lost it. She replaced it with a brass and glass cheapo from Haxford Market. It's why she was murdered. The killer stole it, but they stole the wrong ring."

Another smack in the mouth for her. Unlike Lizzie Finister's, this was metaphorical. When she did speak, it was a hiss. "I'll kill him."

"Not before I've had chance to speak to him, I hope. Right, if you'll just settle the bill, I'll be on my way."

Five minutes later, I came away £80 richer, and sat behind the wheel wondering where to go next.

As it turned out, the phone decided for me.

I was about to start the engine when it rang, number unknown. Many people would not even bother to make the connection, but as a private eye, I couldn't afford to miss any calls.

I swept my finger across the screen and put the phone to my ear. "Christine Capper."

"*The* Christine Capper?" asked a female voice. "Agony aunt and interviewer on Radio Haxford?"

"As of yesterday, ex interviewer and ex agony aunt," I said. "Who am I speaking to?"

The voice came back bubbly, full of

confidence. "Gaynor Armistead. Producer, The Local View. I work for TVYK. I spoked to Eric Reitman about an hour ago and he told me you have a story to tell. Hounded by the press and police for a crime you didn't commit, fired from your job. I'm interested."

"Well, it's not quite that clear cut—"

"What price we can come out, record tomorrow morning and get you on telly tomorrow evening?"

"Well, I, er—"

"Give me your address, girl, and we'll be with you, when...? Ten o'clock in the morning. Is that okay?"

"I, er, I suppose so."

"Great stuff, Christine. Now where do we find you?"

"Seventeen Bracken Close, Haxford. That's south of Huddersfield on the—"

"I know where Haxford is, luv. I'll see you tomorrow morning, Christine. Bye."

And with that, she ended the call leaving my head spinning. If Heath Mottershaw could sell like her, he wouldn't have any problems shifting his fleet of clapped out cars.

Where now, who next, where now, who next? The thoughts whirled round my befuddled brain. I needed to speak to Roger Trippet but I hadn't a clue where to find him, and anyway, Gaynor wossname had knotted my thought processes so badly, I didn't know how I might approach him. Beyond that I still had to confront Ian Noiland and Lizzie Finister, but for the same reason I couldn't handle Trippet, they would make mincemeat of me. Literally in Lizzie's case.

There was nothing else for it but Haxford Mill and a natter with Dennis over a cup of tea in Sandra's Snacky.

I rang ahead and Dennis complained that he was knee deep in rebuilding an engine, but I insisted and by the time I got to the Snacky on the third floor of the mill, he was waiting for me... along with Tony , Lester and Greg.

"What's this?" I asked, as I waited for Sandra to deliver my tea and one of those dinky apple pies Mr Kipling makes. "Are you all on strike, waiting for me to arbitrate?"

"Dennis has told us about your problems, Christine," Tony replied, "and we all wanted to show our solidary with you."

"And norronly us," Dennis said as Sandra approached.

She placed the tea and pie in front of me, yanked a chair from a nearby table, and sat alongside. "I saw the rotten Recorder yesterday afternoon, Chrissy, and if they give you any more grief, you tell Noiland that I'll tell the world just how big a man he isn't when he's horizontal. And as for Finister, send her along and I'll black the other eye."

The men laughed. I didn't. "It's all right, Sandra. I'll deal with them my way." I took a bite from the pie, savoured the sweetness on my tongue, swallowed, and washed it down with a drink of tea. "That's why I had to come here, Dennis. To warn you that I'm on TV tomorrow night."

You could cut the silence with a blunt knife.

That included Sandra, and shutting her up is no mean feat.

"I'll be on The Local View," I said. "Eric Reitman put them onto me, and the producer woman rang me twenty minutes ago. They're coming to our house tomorrow morning so I can spell out exactly what's happened and how badly I've been treated."

If I was a betting woman, I'd have put my money on Dennis being the first to react. And I'd have cleaned up.

A broad grin spread across his face. "You're gonna be on the telly? Hey, will I take the day off?"

"No, you will not," I told him. "I don't want you getting in the way. And it's not the first time, I've been on TV," I reminded him. "Remember when the news people spoke to me that time?"

His humour faded. "I remember. You didn't give us a plug then, did you?"

"No, and you're not going to get one this time, either. Course, if you want to change your Haxford Fixers by-line to something like, 'proprietor, the husband of TV and radio star, Christine Capper' be my guest."

"The only problem being he's not the only proprietor and we're not married to you, Chrissy," Greg said, his index finger darting between Tony, Lester, and himself.

"I was being fly. Dennis will explain he's an expert at it."

Lester disagreed. "Cappy's not in my league."

"Shurrup, Grimy," Dennis complained before focussing on me. "So what are you gonna tell 'em?"

"I'd advise the truth, Christine," Tony said,

"but be careful of what and how you say it. The Recorder and Radio Haxford have plenty of money behind them, and if they decided to sue…" he left the idea hanging in the air.

"Listen to Geronimo," Dennis advised.

"No, Dennis, I don't think so. Finister's photograph was faked, and the police can confirm that. And I have some serious backing at Radio Haxford. Eric Reitman and Reggie Monk have lodged complaints about Langdon and his attitude. I'm going to take a leaf out of your book and tell it like it is." I glanced at my watch. "Right, gentleman, and, er, lady. Can any of you tell me where I might find Roger Trippet? I know he's a benefits adviser, but no one told me where he works."

"I didn't know he did work," Lester said. "Most days you'll find him in the tap room at the Sump Hole."

"In that case, I'll see if I can find him there."

"You just be careful with him," Dennis warned.

"You must know him well, Dennis. He said you service his car."

"Used to. Haven't seen him in a long while. I'm telling you, Chrissy, watch him. He'll be after getting into your pants."

"Wasting his time, luv," I said. "They'll never fit him."

***

The Sump Hole was the local soubriquet for the Engine House pub on Weaver Street, a focal point for most of the town's worst element, including

205

Lester Grimes. Not that Lester was a bad sort, but as an example of his attitude, when he got banned for drink and driving, he had a choice: give up the beer or give up driving. He chose the latter and that precisely summed up the attitude of the Engine House patrons.

Say what you like about Lester, but he was bang on the mark concerning Roger Trippet. When I walked into the pub, crowded with people determined to celebrate Christmas early, I saw him and Heath Mottershaw right away, tucked in at a corner table away from the door. I managed to secure a glass of sparkling water, then fought my way through the crowds again until I stood with them.

"Well, what a coincidence," I gave them my most evil smile. "The very men I need a word with."

If looks could kill, I'd have been on my way to the mortuary.

Mottershaw was the first to respond. "Scram, Capper. We've nowt to say to you."

I glanced around, spotted an empty chair dragged it to their table and sat down. The Sump Hole was known for the fights which regularly broke out, and I didn't feel half as confident as my fake front suggested, but even so, I was not willing to walk away.

"You don't learn, do you, Mr Mottershaw? Didn't you guess from our earlier meeting that I don't go away?"

Trippet glowered. "How about we drag you away and give you what you gave Lizzie Finister?"

"I'd rather you did that, Mr Trippet, than give

me what you usually give tarts like Lizzie Finister."
I put on a sterner, more demanding voice. "Listen to
me, you pair of overgrown idiots. Tomorrow
morning, I'm recording a piece for The Local View,
and it'll go out tomorrow night. My name has been
dragged through the mud for the last few days, and
I'm determined to get my own back. I'm going to
drag everyone else's name into the sewage works,
and that includes you two. By the time I've finished,
you'll be the laughing stock of Haxford and you'll
both be at the top of the police suspect list for
killing Katya Watkins." I rounded on Trippet.
"Especially you."

"Me?" he said, offended, even outraged.

"Yes, you. According to legend, you're the one
with the horizontal skills, and Katya's knickers were
off. Someone, presumably male, or whatever passes
for male with fools like you, had had his way with
her. What happened, Roger? Did she want more
than a quickie on the floor of Barncroft's Farm?
Was she becoming too demanding?"

"Get stuffed."

"The way you stuffed her? I don't think so." I
tapped my temple. "I have a solid, reliable memory.
I need it as a private eye, and I remember you
wearing a stupid chain with a medallion. The police
are looking for the chain that strangled her. Cleared
you, have they? Don't answer that. I know for a fact
they haven't."

He reached out to grab hold of me, but a
dangerous voice stopped him.

"Lay one finger on my mother, Trippet, and I'll
kick you all over town." We all looked up into the

angry eyes of my son.

"She's accusing me of—"

"It's nothing at the side of what I'll do if you touch her." Simon paused a moment. "Mandy Hiscoe wants to see you at the station, and if I have to I'll drag you there. I can always tell them you resisted arrest. If you know what's good for you you'll shift your arse over there now."

His face a mask of impotent fury, Trippet finished his beer and stormed out.

Simon focused on me. "Come on, Mam. Let me get you out of this hell hole."

We fought our way out into the biting fresh air where Simon prepared to give me a lecture.

I cut in before he could say a word. "How did you know I was here?"

"Dad rang me at the station. Mother, what are you doing hassling low life like Trippet and that clown Mottershaw?" He only called me mother when he was annoyed with me.

"I'm trying to find out who killed Katya."

"You've been officially cleared and according to Dad, you're on telly tomorrow slagging everyone off. Katya's killer is our business, Mam, not yours. Leave it to us, and you concentrate on getting ready for Christmas."

I wasn't disposed to argue. "Yes, love," I lied. "I'll do just that."

Chapter Eighteen

Barely the right side of fifty, Gaynor Armistead's dark hair was cut short, more like a 1950s crew cut (not that I'm old enough to remember such styles). The kind of crop you would have associated with a man at one time. She was a little on the heavy side, with large hands and strong wrists, and her brown eyes had a sort of lusty sheen about them which made me feel transparent.

I was up before Dennis left for work on that Wednesday morning, and busy with the Dyson and my other cleaning and polishing equipment as he left.

Not that he let it go without comment. "Who starts cleaning at this time of day?"

"I have people coming and this house is a mess."

"Nah. You want a mess, you should come to our workshop. Now that's a real mess."

"Yes, Dennis, I've seen it. Why don't you pop along there and give it a good clean while I sort the house out?"

With that, he was gone and I set about the work.

Our bungalow would be on TV that evening and I would not allow the houseproud of Yorkshire to look down their noses at me. I hoovered the carpets, mopped the kitchen floor, swept the conservatory, and then set about the furniture with a can of polish and several dusters. I tidied and plumped the cushions in both the front room and the conservatory, then tackled the bedroom, clearing discarded underwear and nightwear into the laundry basket, which I hid in the glory hole cupboard in the kitchen. I scrubbed the kitchen tops clean and put the dirty dishes in the dishwasher, and by nine o'clock, the house sparkled.

I'd barely finished when Mandy rang. "We've released Trippet under interrogation. We don't think it's him, Chrissy. He admitted he'd had his way with Katya on Friday night, but it was a good while before she was killed, and someone almost caught them at it. That's why her pants were off. Instead of putting them back on, she put them in her pocket, and the killer must have been frisking her for Adele's engagement ring."

"And thrown them off to one side? What about the chain and medallion Trippet wore?"

"Not a match for Katya's wounds, but he's still a person of interest. Listen, kiddo, enjoy your fifteen minutes of telly fame. I'll make sure I'm watching."

She rang off and I set about choosing my clothing, a pair of tight-fitting joggers, flouncy, white blouse, and a black cardigan, after which I hopped in the shower, spent ten minutes cleaning myself up, before dressing and settling in front of the bedroom mirror to primp my hair.

I had just decided that I looked every inch the perfect housewife, when the doorbell rang, causing

210

me to check the time. Ten minutes to ten. It couldn't be Gaynor and her crew… could it?

Yes it could.

"Morning, Christine. We're bit early. Not a problem, is it?"

Even if it was, I wouldn't have said so.

In the days when Radio Haxford used to record in the conservatory they came along with a huge crew carrying their electrical bits and pieces in a small pantechnicon… that's a furniture van for those of you who don't know.

At the side of them, Gaynor was short-handed. There was just her, one muscular cameraman with his huge camera, and one sound man with a small electronic board and a couple of radio mikes. She introduced them as Sebastian, the cameraman, and Gil, the sound guy. Both were in their thirties.

I led them through to the conservatory where the interview would be conducted, but Gaynor wanted to see the whole house, first.

"We need some establishing shots," she told me, and she and the cameraman went walkabout with me tagging along like a spare part.

She saw our wedding photographs in the front room and shrugged. "Been married long, Christine?"

"Getting on for thirty years."

"Ugh. Domestic servitude. How do you do it? Never had much time for men personally. Waste of space, time and energy most of them."

"Yes, well, I married one of the best. Honest, faithful and reliable. Now, shall we get a cuppa before we start?"

"Good idea. I need the full back story from you before we get into the interview."

While her two assistants carried on setting up their equipment in the conservatory, Gaynor and I sat at the kitchen table and I told her everything that had gone on since the previous Friday.

Cappy the Cat had kept out of my way all morning, but once we settled down with a brew, he paid us a brief visit. He never cared for the Radio Haxford crew, and he soon lost interest in the TVYK mob when they took no notice of him. One of the two men had the audacity to shoo our temperamental tomcat away, an action that was sure to add him to Cappy the Cat's hit list when cats eventually took over the world.

"So this was all down to the police's initial action in arresting you, was it?" Gaynor asked when I'd finished telling her the tale.

She looked disappointed when I disagreed. "I used to be a police officer, and I won't hear anything said against them. They had a witness. They were duty bound to question me, and DI Quinn did go on TV yesterday morning to formally clear my name. No, Gaynor, the problem was one of the media's making. Now, I know you're in the same business and you probably don't want to hear anything said against them, but that is the situation, and if you're not prepared to let me say what's on my mind, tell it as it really happened, then there's no point in our going any further."

She promptly put me right. "We're a mercenary lot in the media, luv, and I don't really care who you're having a go at. Thing is, are you prepared to

212

name names? I have to warn you, if you name anyone, you need to be able to back it up, or you could drop all of us in the doggy do."

"Yes, I am prepared to name the guilty parties and if you want back up, speak to Eric Reitman. He'll vouch for the way Radio Haxford treated me. As for the local newspaper and their reporter, watch Paddy Quinn on yesterday's local news. It should tell you all you need to know."

"Good on you. I've already seen Quinn's piece. Eric recommended I watch it. We could do with a copy of that newspaper with the fake photograph on the front page."

I left the table, disappeared into the front room where I collected the Recorder from my workstation, made my way back to the kitchen and handed it over.

She looked it over, skim-read it, and turned to the editorial. Once having read that, she closed the newspaper and tapped the photograph of Lizzie Finister. "You didn't do this?"

I shook my head. "I punched her in the mouth, split her lip, but that black eye is either faked or it came from someone else. I have that argument to take up with the Recorder yet."

She leaned back and called to the conservatory. "Seb, get in here, I need a close up still of this newspaper."

Sebastian, the taller of the two men, came in, a digital camera slung round his neck. A good looking, dark-haired hunk, chest muscles straining through his official issue TVYK shirt, the idle thought crossed my mind that most of the time I didn't care for beefcake, but I might make an exception in his case. It's nice to daydream now and then isn't it?

Gaynor handed me the newspaper and I held it up at chest level, and he faffed about with the settings on his camera. "I need to see your fingers holding the paper," he told me as he looked through the viewfinder. He clicked the button once, twice, three times, then accessed the image(s) and passed the camera to his boss. She studied them and nodded her approval.

Handing the camera back, while Sebastian disappeared into the conservatory, she focussed on me.

"After Eric rang yesterday, I listened to some of your slots on the Radio Haxford website. You're good, Christine. Well-spoken, no hesitation, no trace of nerves. But this is TV, not radio, and you might feel a little jittery when we first start. Don't worry about it. We'll probably record about an hour, but we'll only use twenty-five minutes or so. If we need to go over anything, I'll give you the word and we just do it again. Okay?"

I nodded. She downed the rest of her tea in one gulp, reminding me of Lester Grimes's approach to sinking beer, and we made our way to the conservatory where Gil set up the radio mike, dropping the power pack in the back pocket of my joggers and clipping the mike to my cardigan.

I didn't realise it, but Sebastian had put up a couple of lights while we were nattering in the kitchen. "Balance," he explained and waved at the sultry weather outside.

214

I half-grasped the idea. If the sun came out, it would throw the lighting out. Not that there was much danger of the sun putting in an appearance.

"When you do the Christine Capper Interview you're face to face with the subject," Gaynor said. "We don't work like that. We'll concentrate on you, and I'll put the questions to you. They'll be voiceover only. We'll deal with the intro when we get back to the studio. You ready to go, Christine?"

I said nothing. I didn't know enough about the process to argue.

"We'll have a one-minute lead in with no one saying anything, including you," she told me, and again I nodded. And she gave Sebastian the instruction to go.

It was a curious situation, just sitting there, the camera focussed on me, all of us remaining silent. On radio even a one-second gap is like an eternity, and I had to remind myself that this was television. Different media, different set of rules.

And then we were going properly.

"Christine, just to get a little background, you say this all flared up with the murder of a young woman at a Christmas fancy dress ball last week."

Nervous? I was shaking like the house foundations when the builders came to install wheelchair ramps after the attack on Dennis the previous year.

"That's right," I said, "and I freely admit that in the days leading up to the festival ball I had a couple of arguments with the woman in question."

Gaynor gave me the thumbs up and I felt a little more relaxed. A little more? From that point, there

215

was no holding me. I answered every question, every prompt fluently, without hesitation, told the camera (and the viewers) precisely what happened and when, and as I rattled on, I could feel the anger building again.

About three-quarters of an hour after we began, I let it loose when Gaynor asked me to summarise the week just gone.

"The disgraceful behaviour of Lizzie Finister and Ian Noiland, the managing editor of the Haxford Recorder, ensured that I came face to face with James Langdon, the controller of Radio Haxford, who terminated my contract there and then. Even the police said that Finister faked the photograph – and she did – and yet, Noiland ran it. Does he claim he didn't know it was faked? As at this moment in time, he won't speak to me. During the confrontation with Langdon, I was told that guilt and innocence didn't matter. Is that what we've come to in this country? Guilt or innocence are no longer relevant. All that matters is how this kind of issue affects an organisation's reputation. That trio – Noiland, Finister, Langdon – are a disgrace to the freedom the press of this country enjoys. Their attitude, their approach is more suitable to Nazi Germany or communist Russia, and I give them fair warning that Christine Capper will not let them get away with it."

Gaynor allowed a suitable pause after I'd finished speaking, ordered Sebastian to cut the video and then applauded me. "That was brilliant, Christine. Rehearsed?"

"Sort of," I admitted. In fact, I'd spent some

216

time organising my thoughts and rehearsing the closing speech the night before.

"It'll go out tonight at half past six. I just hope you're ready for the flak."

I scowled. "Bring it on."

Chapter Nineteen

Whatever support I could have mustered through my vlog, it was nothing compared to that which followed my appearance on The Local View.

Dennis came home from work early and we watched the programme together, and we both agreed that my performance was not only candid but satisfactory. Gaynor completed the programme voiceover, saying TVYK had contacted the Haxford police who confirmed my eversion of events. Radio Haxford and the Haxford Recorder both declined to comment.

From the moment the programme ended, the phone hardly stopped ringing, and on Thursday morning, my inbox was packed with messages of support. I also learned that the offices of both Radio Haxford and the Recorder saw small groups of protestors complaining about the treatment I had received.

Ian Noiland rang at quarter past nine. He was pleasant, but obviously cowed as he invited me to a meeting to discuss the problems, and I agreed, but only if I could bring Mandy Hiscoe with me, and when I called her, she was ready to sit at my side but she freely admitted she had her own agenda.

Even with her alongside me, I felt more than a

little uncomfortable walking into Ian's office. Even though I was (technically) the injured party, I'd given him, Lizzie, and the Recorder a proper pasting on The Local View, and I guessed he would not take it lying down. Frankly, I'd rather have had my brother, Stephen, acting as my solicitor, with me but he and his wife were still in the Canary Islands.

What did surprise me was that Ian and Lizzie were alone. I'd expected him to have his legal adviser with him, and although he was only mildly welcoming, he nevertheless waved us to seats opposite him and asked if we would like tea or coffee. We both declined.

For her part, Lizzie looked downcast, surly, and guilty. And so she should.

"I'm hoping we can sort this mess out amicably," Ian announced.

I didn't have to say anything. Mandy got there first.

"The ball, Mr Noiland, is in your court." She pointed at Lizzie while still speaking to Ian. "Your reporter not only named Mrs Capper as a suspect, which breaches press and police protocols, and which caused severe distress for her and her family, but Ms Finister also faked her injuries. That could be seen as harassment, or even an attempt to pervert the course of justice should the issue come to court. And you would be on thin ice. Ms Finister, as DI Quinn has already made clear to you, was interviewed by PCs Scott and Keele soon after the assault, and the minor injury she sustained bore no resemblance to the photograph carried on your front page on Monday evening." Mandy paused to let the message sink in. "I'm not here to advise Mrs Capper on her legal rights. Rather, I'm here to assess whether any charges should be brought against Ms Finister and the Haxford Recorder."

I thought Ian would let Lizzie speak, but I was wrong. He held up both hands in a gesture of surrender. "I can't argue with you, Sergeant, but do let me make my position clear. I wasn't working on Sunday, so one of the juniors was the first to see Lizzie. She didn't realise that Lizzie had used theatrical makeup to blacken her eye. Instead she took a photograph. When I saw that on Monday morning I was furious..." He aimed his gaze at me. "With you, Christine. To lash out at a reporter for doing her job—"

"She shouldn't have named me," I interrupted. "And you shouldn't have allowed my name to appear in the article."

"To be strictly accurate, the protocol by which we do not name a suspect is just that. A protocol. An agreement with the police. It is not enshrined in law."

"You cost me my job."

"For which we apologise unreservedly, and I will speak to James Langdon about it." He gave us a thin smile. "He and I play golf together now and again, so I know him quite well."

"I'm so pleased for you," I sneered, "What are you gonna do about her?" I pointed at Lizzie.

"Ms Finister has been disciplined for the fake photograph. She will be suspended without pay until the New Year."

I glowered at her. "But you're still pressing the

220

charges?"

She glared back. "Give me one good reason why I shouldn't?"

"I can't, but I've already shown you up as a liar on local TV, and Gaynor Armistead and Eric Reitman have enough contacts for me to get the story out nationwide. How many rags will want your syndications when that happens?"

"You punched me."

"You got me fired and if I'd known in advance that was going to happen, I'd have done a sight more than smack you in the mouth. I'd have knocked all your flaming teeth out."

"Ladies please—"

"Shut it," I interrupted Ian.

But I couldn't shut Mandy up. "Back off, both of you."

I shut up and Lizzie focused on the view beyond the windows.

Mandy picked up the debate again. "Ms Finister, Lizzie, let me ask, where did you get the information regarding Christine's alleged guilt?"

She glared at Mandy now. "You can get stuffed. I don't reveal my sources."

Mandy's next move took me by surprise, never mind Ian and Lizzie. She got to her feet. "In that case, I'll bid you all good day and I hope you enjoy your time in prison, Lizzie."

I held my breath. Ian almost jumped out of his seat, and Lizzie was on the verge of panic.

"Wait," she pleaded. "What do you mean prison? I can't go to—"

Mandy rounded on her. "At this moment in

time, Ms Finister, you are withholding evidence pertinent to an unlawful killing. Did it ever enter your thick head that once we'd cleared Christine, the person who gave you that information might just be the killer? I want a name, or I'll drag you to the station right now."

She sat silent in her seat, swollen lip pouting, sulk written all over her face.

"Right. Elizabeth Finister, I'm arresting you—"

"Wilma Elmond," Ian interrupted and when we all looked at him, he insisted, "She's the one Lizzie spoke to."

Mandy focussed on Lizzie. "Is that correct?"

Lizzie said nothing, but she gave the slightest nod of her head to agree with Ian.

And in that moment, I suddenly realised everything.

I got to my feet. "Mandy, we need to leave." I faced Ian. "Let me assure you, if Lizzie presses her charges against me, I will go to the law against the Recorder for that fake photograph, and I might get way with a fine, but it'll cost you a hell of a lot more."

Ian gave me an obsequious smile. "Leave it with me, Christine. I'll see what I can do."

Would I have loved to be a fly on the wall in that office after we left? Not half. But I had more important matters on my mind, as I explained to Mandy when we left the building.

"I know what's been going on. I know who killed Katya, and I know why. If you let me tackle it, we'll close the case in half an hour."

222

When we walked in, it was obvious that Wilma was not expecting us and neither did she want to see us.

"Get out. Both of you."

I gave her my most evil smile. "It's not going to happen, Wilma. We know everything… oh, I'm sorry, but you don't know my good friend Detective Sergeant Hiscoe, do you?"

"I know her, and she can—"

"Oh good," I interrupted. "Saves me having to introduce her, doesn't it? So tell me, who were you dressed up as at the ball last Friday?"

She took affront. "I wasn't there."

Mandy stepped in. "Then how could you tell my colleagues and Lizzie Finister that you'd seen Mrs Capper murder Katya Watkins?"

I tutted. "If you'd told me it was her last Saturday, we'd have been that much further forward."

"I couldn't and you know it." Mandy eyed Wilma again. "Mrs Elmond?"

"I... er… All right, so I was dressed as Santa."

I took my irritation out on Wilma. "And Katya didn't recognise you? Mind, I don't suppose anyone would behind the beard. So why did you kill her? Because of the stolen jewellery you sell?"

"I didn't. I never went near her. I saw you throttle her."

I shook my head. "We're not going through that again." I looked down at the glass-topped counter and the costume jewellery, saw what I was looking for, and beckoned Mandy to join me. I pointed out

223

the stirrup hoop. "See that? It's mine. I deliberately left it in the toga when I brought it back the other day." I looked further round the display, until I saw the bracelet. "And if I'm not mistaken, that belongs to Joanne Petheridge. She lost it after hiring a Halloween costume here."

"Let me have a look at them, Mrs Elmond," Mandy insisted.

"I came by these honestly I don't have to—"

"I'd advise you to cooperate, Mrs Elmond. You're in enough trouble as it is. Now let me see them."

Reluctantly, the woman took them out and laid them on the glass top. Mandy picked up the bracelet, screwed up her eyes and read the engraving on the inside. It was so tiny, I was surprised she could read it at all. I don't think I would have managed it.

"To my darling Jo. I love you forever. Bernard." Mandy looked at me and raised her eyebrows.

"Joanne told me about it. Bernard, her husband, bought her that for her fiftieth. Paid a couple of hundred pounds for it. She hired a costume here for a Halloween party, and never saw the bracelet again. I think it got tangled up in the costume, just like my earring."

"Finders keepers," Wilma insisted.

"Stealing by finding actually," I told her. "What efforts have you made to contact the people who 'lost' these items? Answer, none. You certainly haven't rung me regarding that stirrup hoop, and that, Mrs Elmond, is theft. Mandy?"

"Quite right, Christine. And you, Mrs Elmond, are wading in dog poo. Now in order to save yourself from a murder charge, don't you think you should tell us what you really saw on Friday night?"

"Bugger off."

"As you wish. Wilma Elmond, I'm arresting you on suspicion of murder, charges of theft, stealing by finding, and attempting to pervert the course of justice. You do not have to say anything, but if you fail to mention something—"

"I didn't kill her." She was panicking now.

"Then who did?"

Silence.

"Very well," Mandy said. "I'll continue with the caution."

Wilma leapt in again. "I don't know who it was. I was in the lavatory and as I came out, I just saw the back of him and she followed him, going round the side of the old farmhouse. I didn't see who, but I figured they were disappearing for a bit of how's your father in the house."

"That was my opinion too," I said, "but the farmhouse is boarded up. Wouldn't they go into Hattersley Woods for that?"

"Have you ever dropped your clouts in the woods at this time of year? That old house might be nippy, but if they were up for it, they'd get in somehow."

Mandy brought us back on track. "So it was a man you saw her with?"

"I reckon. Course, I didn't really see him, but it coulda been a woman. I didn't know Watkins that well, did I?"

225

"Then why blame Mrs Capper?"

"I think I can explain that, Mandy," I cut in. With a steely eye on Wilma, I demanded, "Where is it? Adele's ring?"

For a moment I thought she was going to deny it. Then she reached beneath the counter, slid open a drawer, brought the ring out and laid it on the glass top.

The frustration settled on Mandy now. "Would someone tell me what is going on?"

"Simple enough," I said. "When I came here to hire the Aphrodite costume, I told her that Adele had hired me to find the ring." I aimed the finger of accusation at Wilma. "She already had it. I'm guessing Heath Mottershaw took it, gave it to Katya as part of a costume and like my earring and Jo's bracelet, when Katya brought it back, the ring was tangled in the folds of the costume." Again I pointed at the woman. "She was worried I'd get there eventually, so when Katya turned up dead, what better way of taking me out of the game than accusing me?"

Some of Wilma's defiance returned when she glared at me. "It's mine as much as it's Adele's."

"But she's the older sister, isn't she, and more entitled?" I felt my temper rising. "Do you know how much damage you've done to me personally?"

"No. Now ask me if I care."

Mandy made a quick call to the station, asking for at least one female officer to come to her assistance, and then, eliminating the suspicion of murder, read the full caution to Wilma. Minutes later, Rehana Suleman and Fliss Keele turned up, handcuffed Wilma and took her away. As we came out into the cold of day, a forensic team turned up and Mandy gave them their orders.

"I want every scrap of clothing and every item of jewellery logged and as far as possible, the real owners identified so we can contact them. After that, you can tape the premises off as a crime scene." She handed over the shop keys." She'll not likely be released before you're finished, so make sure lock up properly." With that, she turned to me. "Well done, Chrissy but we're still no nearer identifying Katya's killer."

"We'll get there, Mandy. Do you need a statement from me regarding Wilma?"

"Shouldn't think so, but we need you to formally identify the earring. And while I think on, you could contact Jo Petheridge for us, tell her to come and identify her bracelet."

"If she'll talk to me."

"Like that, is it?"

"Unfortunately." I sighed. "I'll text her."

We went our separate ways, Mandy to the station, me to the market hall and Terry's place, where I sat with a cup of tea and the inevitable toasted teacake, brooding over the events of the last week and however long. I mean I was brooding not the tea or the teacake.

Disaster was a mild description, but when I thought about it, I had enjoyed some triumphs. I'd tracked down Adele's ring, identified the person who stole Jo's bracelet, and successfully cleared my name of any involvement in the murder of Katya Watkins. But whatever pleasure I could take from

227

all that was offset by two major and unforgiveable errors: thumping Lizzie Finister and all but accusing Jo of Katya's murder. Those two actions had cost me a promising friendship and whatever career I might have had in radio. The latter was compounded by my tell-it-all appearance on The Local View. And to add to my woes, I faced a possible court case courtesy Lizzie, and I never did learn who killed Katya, although that final item was only a matter of personal pride.

Still, I could bring a bit of good news to a couple of people, although, it would be difficult to predict quite how Adele would react to the news that her husband really had handed the ring to Katya (it had to be him) and that her sister stole it.

Jo was another matter altogether. If I rang, she would not answer, so as I said to Mandy, I would have to text her, and it was open to question as to whether she would read any text with my name attached to it.

But not if I worded it right.

The first two words I tapped in were *your bracelet* and after it, I typed, *is with the police after being found amongst other stolen items. You need to identify it. Get in touch with DS Hiscoe at Haxford police station. Chrissy.*

I hesitated a moment, my finger hovering over the 'send' icon, then made up my mind and hit the button. The rest would be up to her.

I didn't claim any responsibility for finding it. Had I done so, she might have read it as an attempt to crawl back into her good books, and Christine Capper did not crawl to anyone... well, not very often.

Having done that, I finished my lunchtime snack, then rang Adele Mottershaw.

"What do you want?"

"Your grandma's ring has turned up and I believe you owe me more money."

"Sod off. I know what happened to it. That cringing coward owned up after you hassled me the other day. Like you said, he loaned it to that bag, Watkins, and she lost it playing silly buggers in Hattersley Woods."

"So you knew what really happened not long after you hired me. Well thanks for nothing. Anyway, you don't know what happened to it afterwards, do you?"

"And you do?"

"I do. And I know where it is right now. Shall we say another fifty?"

"Done."

"I'll be there in twenty minutes."

Chapter Twenty

I don't think Adele was best pleased at handing over another fifty pounds especially when I told her the police had the ring.

"It's evidence," I said, "and they'll probably need you to identify it."

"Evidence of what?"

"Against the person who stole it. That person is your sister. Wilma Elmond."

Well, honestly. I've heard some language in my time, but she used several words I'd never heard before, and it was hardly the way one expects a woman to describe her sister.

When she calmed down I told her everything Wilma had told us, and concluded, "We don't really know who murdered Katya, but I have to say there's a possibility that it was Heath." Before she could shoot me down with even more abusive language, I pressed on. "Can't remember whether I've said it before, but it could be that he was involved in an affair with her."

And she laughed. The kind of braying laugh that sounded more like a donkey in full throe.

"Heath? An affair? Do me a favour. He's forty-four years old and when we met I had to show him what his doings was for."

That brought a spot of colour to my ears and cheeks. "That's a bit too much inf—"

"As a detective you're not up to much are you? Listen to me, missus wonder sleuth. You've just been put through the mill thanks to a pack of lies. Say one word of what I'm going to tell you outside this house, and I'll put you through a kind of hell you daren't imagine."

That ignited my temper. "Don't threaten me, Adele. I might be history at Radio Haxford, but I still have more contacts than the electronic fiddly bits in your smartphone. Now what are you talking about?"

She didn't appear too impressed but she went on in slightly more moderate tones. "Heath is a waste of space horizontally, and Roger Trippet's been keeping me and Katya Watkins and a few others happy for the last god knows how long. Now do like I say and keep it to yourself."

It was hardly a surprise given the opinions of others, including Sandra Limpkin. "He must be a busy man," I commented. "You, Katya, and a few others on top of his job as a benefits advisor, and then the Haxford Larpers. And what about his wife?"

"His wife was history ten years go. And benefits advisor?" She let loose another raucous laugh. "Benefits claimer, more like. Roger hasn't done a day's work in years. That's half the reason his missus left him. That and his habit of putting it about. He lives on the dole and whatever he can beg, steal, or borrow, with the emphasis on the first two. Do me a favour and scram. You've been paid, and

231

the cops'll get the ring back to me so I don't wanna see you again."

Determined not to let her have the last word, I said, "If you ever need a private detective again, Adele, you do me a favour and don't call me." And with that, I walked out.

I might have been a few pounds richer, but I didn't feel any the happier for it as I climbed into the car and took several shunts to turn it round and make for home. It was tempting to say that I hated Heath and Adele Mottershaw, but to hate someone you have to care and I cared nothing for either of them.

It was just after two when I landed, and Cappy the Cat appeared pleased to see me judging from the way he wrapped himself round my legs. It wouldn't last. It never did with him. I put him a feed down, made a cup of tea and settled in the conservatory to watch the turgid sky racing past, delivering flecks of snow as it headed westward.

After Barry Snodgrass's refurbishment and with the addition of the Christmas decorations, the house looked a lot brighter, which was more than could be said for me. True, I had scored a victory on the original case – Adele Mottershaw's missing ring – but at what cost? And it was all thanks to Radio Haxford sending me to the Festival Ball.

There were times when I moaned about the commitment of my minor roles at Radio Haxford, but I would miss the crew; Eric, Reggie, Tom, the sound man, and even dear, sweet, yet gormless Olivia. And what would I do with Tuesdays? The agony aunt slot gave me a reason to get out of bed.

Now I had none. And with the conclusion of the Mottershaw case, I had nothing on the private investigator books. Christmas was four days away and it would be an exciting time partying with friends and family, but January was already looking grim.

I was feeling sorry for myself again, and in an effort to pick up, I began to count the pluses in my life. I had Dennis. I always had Dennis. Mechanically obsessed to the nth degree he might be, but he was a good man, a good husband, and he loved me in his own way. I had Simon and Naomi and of course, the hyperactive Bethany, the darling little girl who meant so much to me. I had Ingrid. She might live the better part of 100 miles from me, but she was still my daughter. Beyond family, I could still count people like Kim, Val Wharrier, and Mandy as good, reliable friends.

And of course, I had my vlog. If my time with Radio Haxford had done nothing else, it had enhanced my viewing figures. There was nothing stopping me from vlogging two days a week instead of the traditional one. In fact, now that I thought about it…

The doorbell rang, bringing an abrupt end to my rambling thoughts.

I wasn't expecting anyone, so I first went to the front room and checked through the window. Jo Petheridge. What did she want? A face to face argument? Or something not so confrontational?

Ready for just about anything, I moved through the hall and opened the door. "Jo?"

She gave me a wan smile and shivered in the

snow flurries. "Hi, Chrissy. Can I come in? It's freezing out here."

Was I that soft or stupid? Well, yes, I was quite frankly. Her whole demeanour suggested repairs to fences.

I stood back, let her in and took her coat. "Go through to the conservatory, I'll make you some tea."

A few minutes later we sat opposite one another, and I took the lead. "On Monday you said if you ever heard from me again it would be too soon."

"Yes, well, things have happened since then, haven't they? I was annoyed, Chrissy I thought you thought I had something to do with Katya's death and I didn't."

"All I really said was you had a window of opportunity. Mandy Hiscoe put me right."

"Interesting. She's not long since put me right, too."

Puzzled? So was I.

She went on to explain. "When I got your text, I went straight to the police station where I identified the bracelet. They told me they're keeping it as evidence in the prosecution against Wilma Elmond. I'll get it back sometime next month. Once the charges have been laid and the CPS okay the prosecution. When I thanked Mandy for finding it, she told me it wasn't her. It was you." Jo paused a moment. "Why didn't you say?"

"After Monday's fiasco? I don't think you'd have listened."

"Probably not."

She giggled and I laughed.

"I was really hoping we could be friends, Chrissy," she said when we had settled again. "And I owe you now."

"I'm for it and you don't owe me anything." I recalled my thoughts on Holmes and Watson, Poirot and Hastings. "You could help me work out who killed Katya, couldn't you?"

Jo frowned. "But surely that's nothing to do with you."

"I've had mud thrown at me, Jo, and it doesn't matter what the cops say, some of it will stick. The best way of making sure everyone knows it wasn't me is to pinpoint the killer and then leave it to Paddy Quinn and Mandy."

"Oh, well, I'm no detective but if I can help, I will." She lapsed into thought for a long moment. "I suppose you found Katya's cheap ring at Wilma's place, too? I remember Kim saying it had been taken from Katya's finger."

The alarm bells rang in my head and the light bulb lit up. "Now that you mention it, no, it wasn't there. That just about clears Wilma, but it still doesn't get us any closer. Wilma insists she saw someone go round the side of the house with Katya, and she assumed it was a man, but it could just as easily have been a woman." Doubt flashed in Jo's eyes and I hurried on to reassure her. "No, I don't mean you." I chewed my lip. "Mind you, we never did ask how the other person was dressed. Excuse me a minute, Jo." I took up my phone and rang Mandy.

"Hey, Chrissy. What can I do for you?"

"I've narrowed the killer down to one of two people," I told her. "Can Wilma remember what the alleged man, woman or other was wearing when she saw them?"

"All she would say was it was too gloomy to see properly, but it was a dark coloured gown, and the person had straggly, black hair."

GOTCHA!

"I'll tell you who it is. Can I come down and watch the interrogation?"

"That'll be up to Paddy. Now who is it?"

When I told her, she was astonished. "Impossible. She wasn't there. We never got a statement with her name on it. We only ever spoke to her because her old man said we should, and that was after he told us that Wilma Elmond had told him you were the murderer."

"No, Mandy, she was there. I saw her, so did Joanne Petheridge and so did Kim Aspinall. In fact, we all spoke to her. What you mean is she'd done a runner before the body was discovered."

"Oh, hell. I see what you mean. Come on down, Chrissy. You'll be handy in the observation room in case she says anything we can't argue with. I'll speak to Paddy once we've brought her in."

***

Mandy always did have ways and means of persuading Paddy, and he was quite happy for me to sit in the observation room with a hook up to his earpiece while they interviewed Adele Mottershaw, who, on the advice of her lawyer, said very little,

236

and when she did talk it was to deny everything.

"I wasn't even there," she lied when first challenged.

I got straight on to Paddy. "She was dressed as Medusa. Kim Aspinall spoke to her and so did I, and I also saw her talking with Katya Watkins earlier in the evening."

Her next mistake came when she pointed the finger at Roger Trippet. "He's the one you should be speaking to. He's always short of money and he knew that she had my grandma's engagement ring. He was probably trying to get it off her so he could hock it."

Once again, I got onto Paddy. "She's right in that Trippet does have dark hair, but he was wearing a long, flowing wig and a short beard and they were both grey."

"Well he was carrying a chain," Adele screamed when Paddy put the point to her. "It was him, I'm telling you. He had it hung round his neck, and you berks missed it."

"No," Mandy argued. "We had him in here and his chain didn't match the wounds to Katya's neck."

The inquisition went on for another hour or more before Paddy finally decided to hold her overnight, despite the protests of her and her lawyer.

"In the meantime, Mrs Mottershaw, we'll get a warrant to search your house and we'll pick up the interview at ten tomorrow morning."

It was noticeable that Paddy let her solicitor leave the building before he joined me in the observation room where he thanked me for my input and told me I wouldn't be needed again until (perhaps) the case came to court.

"I'm certain you're right, Chrissy," he said as I made ready to leave. "It's just a matter of finding the evidence to break her lies down."

In fact it was just after two o'clock on Friday when Mandy rang and told me they'd charged her.

"We checked the dirty green dress she was wearing last Friday night," she told me, "and we found mud on it which could only have come from Barncroft's Farm and the colour of the gown also matches threads we found on Katya's clothing. Better than that, we found the cheap and nasty ring taken from Katya and a set of chains which match the scars on Katya's neck. Kim Aspinall identified the ring and she said she'd also seen Adele wearing the chains on Friday night. When we confronted Adele she finally gave in and told us what happened. Apparently, after she hired you to look for the ring, Heath told her what had happened to it. He loaned it to Katya for their silly LARP games and she misplaced it."

I clucked. "Yes, she told me yesterday that she knew what had happened to the ring right from the start."

"Spot on," Mandy agreed. "She was leading you on to stop you pinning her down for the murder. Anyway, Katya didn't realise it was tangled up in one of the costumes she'd hired from Wilma Elmond. Adele didn't believe it was lost. She thought Katya had kept the ring, so she collared her at the festival ball, dragged her off round the side of the old house where they couldn't be seen. That's when Wilma saw them. Adele hassled Katya, the

238

argument got out of hand, Katya turned to walk away, Adele wrapped the chain round her neck and throttled her, then scarpered before anyone spotted her."

"Just a minute Mandy. Katya's knickers were off. Surely Adele didn't think she'd hidden—"

My favourite detective sergeant cut me off with a tut. "Is your memory fading as you get older? I told you the other day that Trippet and Katya were having fun and games and they almost got caught. Katya didn't have time to put her pants back on. She put them in her pocket. Adele went through those pockets looking for the ring. She was the one who threw the knickers to one side but Katya took them off voluntarily."

And I remembered that Mandy had told me. "It must have taken some time, and I'm surprised they didn't have security round the back there. If they'd been on station, Katya might still be alive."

"Cost cutting according to the organisers. Same old story these days, isn't it? They had security out front and they reckon they'd have noticed anyone sneaking round the side to get in – or out – round the back." Mandy took a breath. "Anyway, it's all signed, sealed and on its way to the CPS, and it's mostly thanks to you, Chrissy."

I accepted the compliment with appropriate humility. "All I wanted was to clear my name… and find Adele's ring. And I'll bet she'll have to pawn that to meet some of her legal bills."

"Her problem not yours, or mine. Anyway, Chrissy, if I don't see you before, have great Christmas."

239

"You too, Mandy. Love to Darlene, and I'll probably see you sometime over the holidays."

Epilogue

Saturday December 23rd dawned grey, sultry, threatening rain, sleet, perhaps even snow, and I should have been on the up having successfully helped pin Adele down, but I was not. I'd lost too much over the last twelve days to feel celebratory.

The mood did not last long. I had far too much to do, including a huge food shop at CutCost and a fair bit of last-minute dashing round town for bits and pieces. And as if that were not enough, it was my mother-in-law's 80th birthday.

Dennis and his partners closed Haxford Fixers down on the Friday and they wouldn't reopen until Wednesday, so at ten in the morning, he and I floated over to see Eunice. She was, of course, pleased to see us, but made it clear that she would be partying with her elderly friends and neighbours for most of the day, and we were not welcome, but she would see us on the twenty-fifth. Would we kindly leave whatever gifts (preferably cash) we'd brought for her and clear off. We left her just after eleven, spent an hour in town, then hit CutCost where the bill almost gave Dennis a heart attack.

"I have a lot of people to feed this weekend, Dennis, and you're the biggest glutton of them all. It costs."

241

"Yeah, but two hundred quid?"

"You want egg and chips for Christmas dinner?"

"No, that's not what I'm saying."

"Then shut up and carry it all to the car."

When we got home at two, I was surprised to find a familiar BMW parked outside our gates. As Dennis reversed into the drive, Eric Reitman and his daughter got out of the saloon, and Olivia rushed to give me a hug.

"It's the best news, Mrs Tapper," she whispered, "but I'm not allowed to tell you."

I had only the vaguest idea what was coming but it would be churlish not to invite them in, so leaving Dennis to bring in all the shopping, I sat with them and provided tea all round in the conservatory.

There was the inevitable small talk (wasn't there always with Eric?) and as I was about to bring him to the point of his visit, my husband joined us.

"Are you all right, Dennis?" Eric asked.

"I was before you turned up. I'm not right happy with the way you treated our lass."

"Now Dennis—"

"No, Chrissy, let's tell it like it is. They wiped their boots on you and after all you did for 'em. It's not right."

"You're perfectly correct, Dennis," Eric said, "but it was nothing to do with me. It was all Langdon and that's why I'm here." He focussed on me. "As I said on... was it Tuesday? We – that is Reggie, myself, and a few others – put our complaints to the board of governors, and as a result

Langdon was officially hauled over the coals yesterday. He's been ordered to reinstate you, and he's under a probationary order. If his approach doesn't change, doesn't improve, he's out. You're back on board, Christine."

I had to consider the prospect. Did I really want to go back to it?

Of course I did.

"There's more," Eric said when I agreed. "Gaynor Armistead was so impressed by your performance on Wednesday that she put a proposition to me. I've already accepted, and she did ask me to ask you." He paused to give his announcement some impact. "How would you like a week in Benidorm?"

I was stunned and cautious. "A week in Benidorm with Gaynor? I'm sorry, Eric, but I'm not that way inclined."

He laughed. "No, you barmpot. Not with Gaynor. The TV people have this idea for a reality show around Valentine's Day. They've asked me to direct and I've accepted. I'm taking Beryl, obviously, and Olivia will be there as my assistant." He paused again. "Gaynor wants you to present it."

Stunned? It was like someone had hit me with an overdose of local anaesthetic. "Me?" I demanded as I recovered.

"Why not?"

"Because I don't do television, Eric. Besides, these reality shows tend to use younger men and women as presenters."

"In most cases, yes, but this involves four couples and the age spread is from – I think – mid-twenties to mid-fifties. Come on, Chrissy, you can do it."

"I don't think so."

"That's what you said about Radio Haxford, but you were an overnight success."

In order to sidestep the question, I asked, "What about you? You're not contracted to Radio Haxford, you're employed by them, so how can you float off to Benidorm for TVYK?"

"I'm entitled to leave and there's nothing in my contact of employment that says I can't work freelance. I'm taking a week's leave to do the job. You're ducking the issue, Chrissy. It pays well, and TVYK will foot the bill for your room and you can take Dennis along. You'd be okay with that, wouldn't you, Dennis?"

My other half grinned. "Not half. Go on, Chrissy. Give it a go. The worst you can do is make a total prat of yourself."

Olivia joined the chorus. "Come on, Justine. I'll be there to mix your cardy and cokes."

I wilted. "All right. No promises but I'll speak to Gaynor."

"Great," Eric enthused. "I'll get her to ring you."

When they left, I sat and chewed on the idea for a good while and eventually came to the conclusion that Dennis was right. The worst that could happen was I'd look a fool, but then I'd been made to look like a villain for the past week, so what did it matter?

That wasn't the only good-ish news I had. At five o'clock, Ian Noiland rang, wished me season's greetings and then announced that Lizzie Finister had been persuaded to drop the charges against me, on pain of dismissal if she didn't.

And that is the whole story. I ran into Christmas in an up mood tainted only by the terrifying thought of appearing on TV sometime in February.

That's all for now. It only remains for me to wish you all the very best for Christmas, and I'll be back with you carrying more tales from Haxford early in the New Year.

THE END

THANK YOU FOR READING. I HOPE YOU HAVE ENJOYED THIS BOOK. WOULD YOU BE KIND ENOUGH TO LEAVE A RATING OR REVIEW ON AMAZON?

The Author

David W Robinson retired from the rat race after the other rats objected to his participation, and he now lives with his long-suffering wife in sight of the Pennine Moors outside Manchester.

Best known as the creator of the light-hearted and ever-popular **Sanford 3rd Age Club Mysteries**, and in the same vein, **Mrs Capper's Casebook**. He also produces darker, more psychological crime thrillers as in the **Feyer & Drake** thrillers and occasional standalone titles.

He, produces his own videos, and can frequently be heard grumbling against the world on Facebook at https://www.facebook.com/davidrobinsonwriter/ and has a YouTube channel at https://www.youtube.com/user/Dwrob96/videos. For more information you can track him down at www.dwrob.com and if you want to sign up to my newsletter and pick up a #FREE book or two, you can find all the details at https://dwrob.com/readers-club/

By the same Author
Mrs Capper's Casebook

Christine Capper is a solid, down to earth Yorkshire lass, witty, plain spoken, but with an innate sense of inquiry (all right, then, she's nosy). She passes her days in the West Yorkshire town of Haxford looking after her long-suffering husband, Dennis, a man with an obsession for all things automotive, and putting him right when he goes wrong, which is more often than not. She takes care of their pet, Cappy the Cat, a feline with attitude, dotes on her granddaughter Bethany, and is openly proud of her son, Simon, now Acting Detective Constable Capper of the Haxford force.

A former police officer, she's Haxford's only trained and licenced private investigator. She's choosy about the cases she takes on but appears destined to be dragged into more serious affairs, during which she passes on her findings to her friend, Detective Sergeant Mandy Hiscoe and Mandy's immediate boss, DI Paddy Quinn, a man who is quite open about his dislike for private eyes.

A series of light-hearted mysteries, laced with Yorkshire grit and wit, Mrs Capper's Casebooks are exclusive to Amazon available for the Kindle and in paperback.

You can find them at:
https://mybook.to/cappseries

The Sanford 3rd Age Club Mysteries

These titles are published and managed by
Darkstroke Books

A decade on from their debut, there are 26 volumes (soon to be 27) and a special in the Sanford 3rd Age Club Mystery series.

We follow the travels and trials of amateur sleuth Joe Murray and his two best friends, Sheila Riley and Brenda Jump. The short, irascible Joe, proprietor of The Lazy Luncheonette in Sanford, West Yorkshire, jollied along by the bubbly Brenda and Sheila, but only his friends, but also his employees, all three leading lights in the Sanford 3rd Age Club (STAC for short). And it seems that wherever they go on their outings on holidays in the company of the born-again teenagers of the 3rd Age Club, they bump into… MURDER.

A major series of whodunits marinated in Yorkshire humour, they are exclusive to Amazon and you can find them at: **https://mybook.to/stac**

Other Works

I also turn out darker works such as The Anagramist and The Frame with Chief Inspector Samantha Feyer and civilian consultant Wesley Drake, and the standalone The Cutter.

For details visit https://dwrob.com/the-dark/

Free Books

Like what you've seen so far? Why to subscribe to my newsletter? I guaranteed that you will not be inundated with emails, and your address will never be sold on. Once you sign up, you will receive details of to one but TWO free novellas.

For more information visit
https://dwrob.com/readers-club/

Printed in Great Britain
by Amazon